Once Valentina s

had, she would s l.
Luca knew she w ,
begging for him to rescue her family from the nightmare of her mother's making.

He was closer than he thought.

He saw the colour of her eyes in the golden light from a window across the canal. Amber eyes and hair shot with golden lights—she might have lost weight, she might have been travelling for more than a day and the skin under her eyes tired, but the intervening years had been good to her. She was more beautiful than he remembered.

And he hungered for her.

But she would soon come crawling.

And he would have her.

All about the author...
Trish Morey

TRISH MOREY wrote her first book at age eleven for a children's book-week competition. Entitled *Island Dreamer,* it told the story of an orphaned girl and her life on a small island at the mouth of south Australia's Murray River. *Island Dreamer* also proved to be her first rejection—her entry was disqualified. Shattered and broken, she turned to a life where she could combine her love of fiction with her need for creativity—Trish became a chartered accountant! Life wasn't all dull, though, as she embarked on a skydiving course, completing three jumps before deciding that she'd given her fear of heights a run for its money.

Meanwhile, she fell in love and married a handsome guy who cut computer code and Trish penned her second book—the totally riveting *A Guide to Departmental Budgeting*—while working for the N.Z. Treasury.

Back home in Australia, after the birth of their second daughter, Trish spied an article saying that Harlequin® was actively seeking new authors. It was one of those eureka moments—Trish was going to be one of those authors!

Eleven years after reading that fateful article (actually June 18, 2003, at 6:32 p.m!), the magical phone call came and Trish finally realized her dream.

According to Trish, writing and selling a book is a major life achievement that ranks right up there with jumping out of an airplane and motherhood. All three take commitment, determination and sheer guts, but the effort is so very, very worthwhile.

Trish now lives with her husband and four young daughters in a special part of south Australia, surrounded by orchards and bushland and visited by the occasional koala and kangaroo.

You can visit Trish at her website, www.trishmorey.com, or drop her a line at trish@trishmorey.com.

Other titles by Trish More available in ebook:

Harlequin Presents®

3093—THE SHEIKH'S LAST GAMBLE *(Desert Brothers)*
3087—DUTY AND THE BEAST *(Desert Brothers)*
3045—FIANCÉE FOR ONE NIGHT

Trish Morey

BARTERING HER INNOCENCE

Recycling programs for this product may not exist in your area.

ISBN-13: 978-0-373-13121-1

BARTERING HER INNOCENCE

This edition published by arrangement with Harlequin Books S.A.

For questions and comments about the quality of this book, please contact us at CustomerService@Harlequin.com.

Printed in U.S.A.

BARTERING HER INNOCENCE

To Jacqui, Steph, Ellen and Claire,

Four gorgeous girls who have grown up amidst the mess and chaos and deadline-mania of a writer's life, and who somehow still managed to turn out all right.

I am so proud of the beautiful, talented, warm and wonderful young women you have become.

I am so looking forward to seeing all that you can be.

juv nun

xxx

CHAPTER ONE

THE last time Tina Henderson saw Luca Barbarigo, he was naked. Gloriously, unashamedly, heart-stoppingly naked. A specimen of virile masculine perfection—if you discounted the violent slash of red across his rigid jaw.

As for what had come afterwards…

Oh God. It was bad enough to remember the last time she'd seen him. She didn't want to remember *anything* that came after that. She must have misheard. Her mother could not mean *that man.* Life could not be that cruel. She clenched a slippery hand harder around the receiver, trying to get a better grip on what her mother was asking.

'Who…who did you say again?'

'Are you listening to me, Valentina? I need you to talk to Luca Barbarigo. I need you to make him see reason.'

Impossible. She'd told herself she'd never see him again.

More than that. She'd *promised* herself.

'Valentina! You have to come. I need you here. Now!'

Tina pinched the bridge of her nose between her fingers trying to block the conflicting memories—the images that were seared on her brain from the most amazing night of her life, the sight of him naked as he'd risen from the bed, all long powerful legs, a back that could have been sculpted in marble, right down to the twin dimples at the base of his spine—and then the mix master of emotions, the anger and turmoil—the anguish and despair—for what had come afterwards.

She pinched harder, seeking to blot out the dull ache in her womb, trying to direct her shocked emotions into anger. And she was angry, and not just about what had happened in the past. Because how typical was it that the first time her mother actually called her in more than a year, it wasn't to wish her a belated happy birthday, as she'd foolishly imagined, but because Lily needed something.

When did Lily not need something, whether it was attention, or money or adulation from a long and seemingly endless line of husbands and lovers?

And now she foolishly imagined Tina would drop everything and take off for Venice to reason with the likes of Luca Barbarigo?

Not a chance.

Besides, it was impossible. Venice was half a world away from the family farm in Australia where she was also needed right now. No, whatever disagreement her mother had with Luca Barbarigo, she was just going to have to sort it out for herself.

'I'm sorry,' she began, casting a reassuring glance towards her father across the room to signal everything was under control. A call from Lily put everyone on edge. 'But there's no way I can—'

'But you have to do something!' her mother shrieked down the telephone line, so loud that she had to hold the receiver away from her ear. 'He's threatening to throw me out of my home! Don't you understand?' she insisted. 'You have to come!' before following it with a torrent of French, despite the fact that Lily D'Areincourt Beauchamp was English born and bred. The language switch came as no surprise—her mother often employed that tactic when she wanted to sound more impassioned. Neither was the melodrama. As long as she had known Lily, there was always melodrama.

Tina rolled her eyes as the tirade continued, not bothering to keep up and tired of whatever game her mother was playing, suddenly bone weary. A long day helping her father bring in the sheep in preparation for shearing wasn't about to end any time soon. There was still a stack of washing up waiting for her in the kitchen sink and that was before she could make a start on the piles of accounts that had to be settled before her trip to town tomorrow to see the bank manager. She rubbed her brow where the start of a headache niggled. She always hated meetings with their bank manager. She hated the power imbalance, the feeling that she was at a disadvantage from the get go.

Though right now the bank manager was the least of her problems…

Across the room Tina's father put down his stock journal on the arm of his chair where he'd been pretending to read and threw her a sympathetic smile before disappearing into the large country kitchen, no real help at all. But then, he'd broken ties with Lily almost twenty-five years ago now. It might not have been a long marriage but, knowing her mother, he'd more than served his time.

She was aware of the banging of the old water pipes as her father turned on the tap, followed by the thump of the kettle on the gas cooker and still her mother wasn't through with pleading her case. 'Okay, Lily,' she managed while her mother drew breath. 'So what makes you think Luca Barbarigo is trying to throw you out of the palazzo? He's Eduardo's nephew after all. Why would he threaten such a thing? And in English, please, if you don't mind. You know my French is rusty.'

'I *told* you that you need to spend more time on the Continent,' her mother berated, switching grievances as seamlessly as she switched languages, 'instead of burying yourself out there in the Australian outback.'

'Junee is hardly outback,' she argued of the mid-sized New South Wales town that was less than two hours from the semi-bright lights of Canberra. Besides, she hadn't exactly *buried* herself out here, more like she'd made a tactical withdrawal from a world she wanted no further part in. And then, because she was still feeling winded by her mother's demands, she added, 'It's quite civilised actually. There's even talk of a new bowling alley.'

Silence greeted that announcement and Tina imagined her mother's pursed lips and pinched expression at her daughter's inability to comprehend that in order to be considered civilised, a city needed at least half a dozen opera theatres, preferably centuries old, at a bare minimum.

'Anyway, you still haven't explained what's going on. Why is Luca Barbarigo threatening to throw you out? What kind of hold could he possibly have over you? Eduardo left you the palazzo, didn't he?'

Her mother fell unusually quiet. Tina heard the clock on the mantel ticking; heard the back door creak open and bang shut as her father went outside, probably so he didn't have to hear whatever mess Lily was involved in now. 'Well,' she said finally, her tone more subdued, 'I may have borrowed some money from him.'

'You what?' Tina squeezed her eyes shut. Luca Barbarigo had a reputation as a financier of last resort. By all accounts he'd built a fortune on it, rebuilding the coffers of his family's past fortune. She swallowed. Of all the people her mother could borrow from, of all the contacts she must have, and she had to choose *him*! 'But why?'

'I had no choice!' her mother asserted. 'I had to get the money from somewhere and I assumed that being family he'd take care of me. He promised he'd take care of me.'

He'd taken care of her all right. And taken advantage into the deal. 'You had to get money for what?'

'To live, of course. You know Eduardo left me with a fraction of the fortune he made out that he had.'

And you've never forgiven him for it. 'So you borrowed money from Luca Barbarigo and now he wants it back.'

'He said if I couldn't pay him, he'd take the palazzo.'

'How much money are we talking about?' Tina asked, pressure building in her temples. The centuries-old palazzo might be just off the Grand Canal, but it would still be worth millions. What kind of hold did he have over her? 'How much do you owe him?'

'Good God, what do you take me for? Why do you even have to ask?'

Tina rubbed her forehead. 'Okay. Then how can he possibly throw you out?'

'That's why I need you here! You can make him understand how unreasonable he is being.'

'You don't need me to do that. I'm sure you know plenty of people right there who can help.'

'But he's *your* friend!'

Ice snaked down Tina's spine. *Hardly friends.* In the kitchen the kettle started to whistle, a thin and shrill note and perfectly in tune with her fractured nerves and painful memories. She'd met Luca just three times in her life. The first in Venice at her mother's wedding, where she'd heard his charming words and felt the attraction as he'd taken her hand and she'd decided in an instant that he was exactly the kind of charming, good-looking rich man that her mother would bend over backwards to snare and that she wanted no part of. And when he'd asked her to spend the night with him, she'd told him she wasn't interested. After all, Lily might be her mother, but no way was Tina her mother's daughter.

The second time had been at Eduardo's seventieth birthday, a lavish affair where they'd barely done more than exchange pleasantries. Sure, she'd felt his eyes burn into her flesh and set her skin to tingling as they'd followed her progress around the room, but he'd kept his distance and she'd celebrated that fact, even if he hadn't given her the satisfaction of turning him down again. But clearly her message had struck home.

The third had been at a party in Klosters where she'd been celebrating a friend's birthday. She'd had one too many glasses of champagne and her guard was down and Luca had appeared out of the crowd and suddenly his charm was infectious and he was warm and amusing and he'd taken her aside and kissed her and every shred of self-preservation she'd had had melted away in that one molten kiss.

One night they'd spent together—one night that had ended in disaster and anguish and that could never be blotted from her mind—one night that she'd never shared with her mother. 'Who said we were friends?'

'He did, of course. He asked after you.'

Bastard! As if he cared. He had never cared. 'He lied,' she said, the screaming kettle as her choir. 'We were never friends.'

Never were.

Never could be.

'Well,' her mother said, 'maybe that's preferable under the circumstances. Then you'll have nothing to risk by intervening on my behalf.'

She put a hand to her forehead, certain the screaming must be coming from somewhere inside her skull. 'Look, Lily, I don't know what good I can do. There is no way my being there will help your cause. Besides, I can't get away.

We're about to start shearing and Dad really needs me here right now. Maybe you'd be better off engaging a lawyer.'

'And just how do you think I'll be able to afford to pay for a lawyer?'

She heard the back screen door slam and her father's muttered curse before the screaming abruptly tapered off. She shook her head. 'I really don't know.' And right now she didn't care. Except to ensure she didn't have to go. 'Maybe…maybe you could sell one or two of those chandeliers you have.' God knew, from the last time she'd visited, it seemed her mother had enough of them to fill a dozen palazzos. Surely if she owed a bit of money she could afford to dispense with one or two?

'Sell my Murano glass? You must be mad! It's irreplaceable! Every piece is individual.'

'Fine, Lily,' she said, 'it was just a suggestion. But under the circumstances I really don't know what else I can suggest. I'm sorry you're having money troubles, but I'm sure I'd be no help at all. And I really am needed here. The shearers arrive tomorrow, it's going to be full-on.'

'But you have to come, Valentina! You must!'

Tina put the phone down and leaned on the receiver a while, the stabbing pain behind her eyes developing into a dull persistent throb. Why now? Why him? It was likely her mother was exaggerating the seriousness of her money problems—she usually managed to blow any problem right out of proportion—but what if this time she wasn't? What if she was in serious financial trouble? And what could she do about it? It wasn't likely that Luca Barbarigo was going to listen to her.

Old friends? What was he playing at? Ships that crashed in the night would be closer to the mark.

'I take it your mother wasn't calling to wish you a happy

birthday, love?' Her father was standing in the kitchen doorframe, a mug of coffee wrapped in each of his big paw-like hands.

She smiled, in spite of the heaviness of her heart and the sick feeling in her gut. 'You got that impression, huh?'

He held up one of the mugs in answer. 'Fancy a coffee? Or maybe you'd like something stronger?'

'Thanks, Dad,' she said, accepting a mug. 'Right now I'd kill for a coffee.'

He took a sip. Followed it with a deep breath. 'So what's the latest in Circus Lily then? The sky is falling? Canals all run dry?'

She screwed up her face. 'Something like that. Apparently someone's trying to throw her out of the palazzo. It seems she borrowed money from Eduardo's nephew and, strangely enough, he wants it back. Lily seems to think I can reason with him—maybe work out some more favourable terms.'

'And you don't?'

She shrugged her shoulders, wishing she could just as easily shrug off memories of a man who looked better naked than any man had a right to, especially when he was a man as cold and heartless as he'd turned out to be. Wishing she could forget the aftermath… 'Let's just say I've met the man.' *And please don't ask me how or when.* 'I told her she'd be better off engaging a lawyer.'

Her dad nodded then and contemplated his coffee and Tina figured she'd put a full stop on the conversation and remembered the dishes still soaking and the accounts still to be paid. She was halfway to the sink when her father said behind her, 'So when do you leave?'

'I'm not going,' she said, her feet coming to a halt. I don't want to go. *I can't go.* Even though she'd told her mother she'd think about it, and that she'd call her back, when she'd never had any intention of going. She'd promised herself she'd never have to see him again and that was a promise she couldn't afford to break. Just thinking about what he'd cost her last time… 'I can't go and leave you, Dad, not now, not with the shearing about to start.'

'I'll manage, if you have to go.'

'How? The shearers start arriving tomorrow. Who's going to cook for a dozen men? You can't.'

He shrugged as the corners of his mouth turned up. 'So I'll go to town and find someone who can cook. You never know, I hear Deidre Turner makes a mean roast. And she might jump at the chance to show off her pumpkin scones to an appreciative audience.' His smile slipped away, his piercing amber eyes turning serious. 'I'm a big boy, Tina, I'll manage.'

Normally Tina would have jumped at her father's mention of another woman, whatever the reason—she'd been telling him for years he should remarry—but right now she had more important things on her mind—like listing all the reasons she couldn't go.

'You shouldn't have to manage by yourself! Why waste the money on flights—and on paying someone to cook—when we're already begging favours from the bank manager as it is? And you know what Lily's like—look at how she made such a drama about turning fifty! Anyone would have thought her life was coming to an end and I bet this is exactly the same. I bet it's all some massively overblown drama, as per usual.'

Her father nodded as if he understood, and she felt a surge of encouragement. Because of course her father would understand. Hadn't he been married to the woman? He, more than anyone, knew the drama queen stunts she was capable of pulling to get her way.

Encouragement had almost turned to relief, and she

was more than certain he would agree. Until he opened his mouth.

'Tina,' he said, rubbing the stubble of his shadowed jawline, 'how long is it since you've seen your mum? Two years? Or is it three? And now she needs you, for whatever reason. Maybe you should go.'

'Dad, I just explained—'

'No, you just made an excuse.'

She stiffened her shoulders, raising her chin. Maybe it was an excuse, and if her father knew the truth, surely he would understand, surely he would be sympathetic and not insist she go. But how could she tell him when she had kept it secret for so long? Her shameful secret. How could she admit to being as foolish and irresponsible as the woman she'd always told herself she was nothing like? It would kill him. It would kill her to tell him.

And when defence wasn't an option, there was always attack…

'So why are you so keen to ship me off to the other side of the world to help Lily? It's not like she ever did you any favours.'

He wrapped an arm around her shoulders and hauled her close, holding her just long enough for her to breathe in his familiar earthy farm scent. 'Who says I'm keen? But she's still your mum, love, and whatever happened between the two of us, you can't walk away from that. Now,' he said, putting his mug down to pick up a tea towel, 'what's this about a new bowling alley in town? I hadn't heard that.'

She screwed up her nose and snatched the tea towel out of his hands, not because she couldn't do with the help or his company, but because she knew he had his own endless list of chores to finish before he could collapse into bed, and partly too because she feared that if he lingered, if he asked her more about her mother's predicament and how she knew the man Lily owed money to, she wouldn't know how to answer him honestly. 'How about that?' she said much too brightly as she pushed him towards the door. 'Neither had I.'

He laughed in that deep rumbling way he had and that told her he knew exactly what she'd been doing. 'Your mum's not going to know what hit her.'

'I'm not going, Dad.'

'Yes, you are. We can check about flights when we go into town tomorrow.' And he came back and hugged her, planting a kiss on her strawberry-blonde hair the same way he'd done ever since she was old enough to remember and probably long before. 'Goodnight, love.'

She thought about her father's words after he'd gone, as she chased cutlery around the sudsy sink. Thought with a pang of guilt about how long it had been since she'd seen her mother. Thought about how maybe her father might be right.

Because even though they'd never seen eye to eye, even though they never seemed to be on the same wavelength, maybe she couldn't walk away from her mother.

And neither did she have to run from Luca Barbarigo.

She had been running. She'd run halfway around the world to forget the biggest mistake of her life. She'd run halfway around the world to escape.

But some mistakes you couldn't escape.

Some mistakes followed you and caught up with you when you least expected it.

And some mistakes came with a sting in the tail that made you feel guilty for wishing things had been different. They were the worst mistakes of all, the ones that kept on hurting you long, long after the event.

She pulled the plug and stood there, watching the suds gurgle down the sink, suds the very colour of the delicate iron lace-work that framed a tiny grave in a cemetery in far distant Sydney.

Tears splashed in the sink, mixing with the suds, turning lacy bubbles pearlescent as they spun under the thin kitchen light. She brushed the moisture from her cheeks, refusing to feel sorry for herself, feeling a steely resolve infuse her spine.

Why should she be so afraid of meeting Luca again? He was nothing to her really, nothing more than a one-night stand that had ended in the very worst kind of way. And if Luca Barbarigo was threatening her mother, maybe Lily was right; maybe she was the best person to stand up to him. It wasn't as if there was a friendship in the balance. And it certainly wasn't as if she was going to be charmed by him.

Not a second time.

She wasn't that stupid!

CHAPTER TWO

SHE was coming.

Just as her mother had said she would.

Luca stood at the darkened balcony overlooking the Grand Canal, his senses buzzing with the knowledge, while even the gentle slap of waters against the pilings seemed to hum with anticipation.

Valentina was coming to save her mother. Expecting to rescue her from the clutches of the evil banker.

Just as he'd intended.

A smile tugged at his lips.

How fortuitous that her mother was a spendthrift with a desperate need for cash. So desperate that she was not bothered to read the terms of any loan agreement too closely. How naive of her to assume that marrying his uncle somehow made her eligible for special treatment.

Special treatment indeed.

And now the noose he'd tied was so tight around the neck of the former beauty that she was about to lose her precious palazzo from beneath her once well-heeled feet.

A water taxi prowled by, all sleek lines and polished timbers, the white shirt of the driver standing out in the dark night, before both taxi and driver disappeared down one of the side canals. He watched the wake fan out across the dark canal and felt the rhythm of water resonate in the beat of his blood; heard it tell him that the daughter was drawing ever closer.

He searched the night sky, counting down the hours, imagining her in the air, imagining her not sleeping because she knew he would be here in Venice, waiting for her to arrive.

Waiting.

He smiled, relishing a sense of anticipation that was almost delicious.

It was delicious.

He was no gambler. Luck was for suckers. Instead he thrived on certainty and detail and left nothing to chance. His version of luck happened when excellent preparation met with sublime opportunity.

The seeds for both had been sown, and now it was time to reap the harvest.

The palazzo had been his uncle's once, before that woman had stuck her steely claws into him and hung on tight, and now it was as good as back in the family fold again. But the satisfaction of returning the palazzo to the family fold was not what drove him now. Because Lily Beauchamp had something far more valuable that he wanted.

Her precious daughter.

She'd walked out on him once. Left the mark of her hand bright on his jaw and walked away, as if she'd been the one on high moral ground. At the time he'd let her go. Waved good riddance. The sex had been good but no woman was worth the angst of chasing her, no matter how good she was in bed.

He'd put her from his mind.

But then her mother had called him, asking for help with the mire of her finances, and he'd remembered the daughter and a night of sex with her that had ended way too prematurely. He'd been only too happy to help then. It was the least he could do for his uncle's widow, he'd told her, realising there might be a way to redress the balance.

So now fate was offering him the chance to right two wrongs. To get even.

Not just with the spendthrift mother.

But with the woman who thought she was different. Who thought herself somehow better.

He'd show her she was not so different to her mother after all. He'd show her he was nobody to walk away from.

And then he'd publicly and unceremoniously dump her.

CHAPTER THREE

ARRIVING in Venice, Tina thought, was like leaving real life and entering a fairy tale. The bustling Piazzale Roma where she waited for her bag to be unloaded from the airport bus was the full stop on the real world she was about to leave behind, a world where buildings were built on solid ground and transport moved on wheels; while the bridges that spanned out from the Piazzale crossing the waterways were the 'once upon a time' leading to a fairy tale world that hovered unnaturally over the inky waters of the lagoon and where boats were king.

Beautiful, it was true, but as she glanced at the rows of windows looking out over the canals, right now it almost felt brooding too, and full of mystery and secrets and dark intent…

She shivered, already nervous, feeling suddenly vulnerable. Why had she thought that?

Because he was out there, she reasoned, her eyes scanning the buildings that lined the winding canal. Luca was out there behind a window somewhere in this ancient city.

Waiting for her.

Damn. She was so tired that she was imagining things.

Except she'd felt it on the plane too, waking from a restless sleep filled with images of him. Woken up feeling almost as if he'd been watching her.

Just thinking about it made her skin crawl all over again.

She pushed her fringe back from her eyes and sucked in air too rich with the scent of diesel fumes to clear her head. God, she was tired! She grunted a weary protest as she hauled her backpack over her shoulder.

Forget about bad dreams, she told herself. Forget about fairy tales that started with once upon a time. Just think about getting on that return plane as soon as possible. That would be happy ending enough for her.

She lined up at the vaporetto station to buy a ticket for the water buses that throbbed their way along the busy canals. A three-day pass should be more than adequate to sort out whatever it was her mother couldn't handle on her own. She'd made a deal with her father that she'd only come to Venice on the basis she'd be back at the farm as soon as the crisis was over. She wasn't planning on staying any longer. It wasn't as if this was a holiday after all.

And with any luck, she'd sort out her mother's money worries and be back on a plane to Australia before Luca Barbarigo even knew she was here.

She gave a snort, the sound lost in the crush of tourists laden with cameras and luggage piling onto the rocking water bus. Yeah, well, maybe that was wishful thinking, but the less she had to do with him, the better. And no matter what her frazzled nerves conjured up in her dreams to frighten her, Luca Barbarigo probably felt the same way. She recalled the vivid slash of her palm across his jaw. They hadn't exactly parted on friendly terms after all.

Tourists jockeyed and squirmed to get on the outer edge of the vessel, cameras and videos at the ready to record this trip along the most famous of Venice's great waterways, and she let herself be jostled out of the way, unmoved by the passing vista except to be reminded she was on Luca Barbarigo's patch; happy to hide in the centre of the boat under cover where she couldn't be observed. Crazy, she knew, to feel this way, but she'd found there were times that logic didn't rule her emotions.

Like the time she'd spent the night with Luca Barbarigo.

Clearly logic had played no part in that decision.

And now once again logic seemed to have abandoned her. She'd felt so strong back home at the kitchen sink, deciding she could face Luca again. She'd felt so sure in her determination to stand up to him.

But here, in Venice, where every second man, it seemed, had dark hair or dark eyes and reminded her of him, all she wanted to do was hide.

She shivered and zipped her jacket, the combined heat from a press of bodies in the warm September air nowhere near enough to prevent the sudden chill descending her spine.

Oh God, she needed to sleep. That was all. Stopovers in Kuala Lumpur and then Amsterdam had turned a twenty-two hour journey into more like thirty-six. She would feel so much better after a shower and a decent meal. And in a few short hours she could give in to the urge to sleep and hopefully by morning she'd feel halfway to normal again.

The vaporetto pulled into a station, rocking sideways on its own wash before thumping against the floating platform and setting passengers lurching on their straps. Then the vessel was secured and the gate slid open and one mass of people departed as another lot rushed in, and air laced with the sour smell of sweat and diesel and churned canal water filled her lungs.

Three days, she told herself, as the vessel throbbed into life and set course for the centre of the canal again, missing an oncoming barge seemingly with inches to spare. She could handle seeing Luca again because soon she would be going home.

Three short days.

She could hardly wait.

The water bus heaved a left at the Canale di Cannaregio and she hoisted her pack from the pile of luggage in the corner where he'd stashed it out of the way. And this time she did crane her neck around and there it was just coming into view—her mother's home—nestled between two well-maintained buildings the colour of clotted cream.

She frowned as the vaporetto drew closer to the centuries-old palazzo. Once grand, her mother's house looked worse than she remembered, the once soft terracotta colour faded and worn, and with plaster peeling from the walls nearly up to the first floor, exposing ancient brickwork now stained yellow with grime at the water level. Pilings out the front of a water door that looked as if it had rusted shut stood at an angle and swayed as the water bus passed, and Tina winced for the once grand entrance, now looking so sad and neglected, even the flower boxes that had once looked so bright and beautiful hanging empty and forlorn from the windows.

Tourists turned their cameras away, searching for and finding more spectacular targets, an old clock tower or a passing gondola with a singing gondolier, and she almost felt ashamed that this was her mother's house, such an unworthy building for a major thoroughfare in such a beautiful city.

And she wondered what her mother could have done with the money she had borrowed. She'd said she'd needed the money to live. Clearly she hadn't spent much of it on returning the building to its former glory. She disembarked at the next stop, heading down one of the narrow *calles* leading away from the canal. The palazzo might boast its own water door but, like so many buildings fronting the canals, pedestrian access was via a rear courtyard, through an ornate iron gate in yet another steeply walled lane, squeezing past clumps of strolling tourists wearing their cruise ship T-shirts and wielding cameras and maps, or being overtaken by fast moving locals who knew exactly where they wanted to go and how to get there in the shortest possible time.

For a moment she thought she'd found the right gate, but ivy rioted over the wall, unkempt and unrestrained, the ends tangling in her hair, and she thought she must have made a mistake. Until she peered closer through the grille and realised why it looked so wrong.

She remembered the courtyard garden being so beautifully maintained, the lawns mowed, the topiary trees trimmed to perfection, but the garden looked neglected and overgrown, the plants spilling from the fifteenth century well at its centre crisp and brown, the neat hedge along the pathway straggly and looking as if it hadn't been clipped for months. Only two bright pots spilling flowers atop the lions guarding the doorway looked as if anyone had made an effort.

Oh, Lily, she thought, looking around and mourning for what a sanctuary this garden had once been. What had happened to let it go like this?

There was no lock on the gate, she realised, the gate jammed closed with rust, and she wondered about her mother living alone, or nearly alone in such a big house. But the gate scraped metal against metal and creaked loudly as she swung it open, a sound that would no doubt frighten off any would-be thief.

It wasn't enough to bring her mother running, of course—Lily was too much a lady to run—but Carmela, the housekeeper, heard. She bustled out of the house rubbing her hands on her apron. Carmela, who she'd met a mere handful of times, but greeted her now with a smile so wide she could have been her own daughter returning home.

'Valentina, *bella*! You have come.' She took her face between her hands and reached up to kiss each cheek in turn before patting her on the back. 'Now, please…' she said, wresting her backpack from her. 'I will take this. It is so good you have come.' A frown suddenly came from nowhere, turning her face serious. 'Your mother, she needs you. Come, I take you.'

And then she smiled again and led the way into the house, talking nonstop all the time, a mixture of English and Italian but the meaning perfectly clear. And Tina, who had been on edge the entire flight, could finally find it in herself to smile. Her mother would no doubt treat her daughter's attendance upon her as her God-given right; Luca Barbarigo would probably see it as a necessary evil, but at least someone seemed genuinely pleased to see her.

She followed Carmela across the threshold and, after the bright autumn sunshine, the inside of the house was dark and cool, her mother still nowhere to be seen. But, as her eyes adjusted, what little light there was seemed to bounce and reflect off a thousand surfaces.

Glass, she realised, remembering her mother's passion for the local speciality. Only there seemed to be a lot more of it than she remembered from her last visit.

Three massive chandeliers hung suspended from the ceiling of the passageway that ran the length of the building, the mosaic glass-framed mirrors along the walls making it look as if there was at least a dozen times that. Lily blinked, trying to stick to the centre of the walkway where there was no risk of upsetting one of the hall tables, also heavily laden with objets d'art, trying to remember what this hallway had looked like last time she was here. Certainly less cluttered, she was sure.

Carmela led her through a side door into her kitchen that smelt like heaven, a blissful combination of coffee and freshly baked bread and something savoury coming from the stove, and where she was relieved to see the only reflections came from the gleaming surfaces, as if the kitchen was Carmela's domain and nothing but the utilitarian and functional was welcome.

The older woman put down Tina's pack and wrapped her pinny around the handle of a pan on the stove. 'I thought you might be hungry, *bella*,' she said, placing a steaming pan of risotto on a trivet.

Tina's stomach growled in appreciation even before the housekeeper sliced two fat pieces of freshly baked bread and retrieved a salad from the refrigerator. After airline food it looked like a feast.

'It looks wonderful,' she said, pulling up a chair. 'Where's Lily?'

'She had some calls to make,' she said, disapproval heavy in her voice as she ladled out a bowl of the fragrant mushroom risotto and grated on some fresh parmigiano. 'Apparently they could not wait.'

'That's okay,' Tina said, not really surprised. Of course her mother would have no compunction keeping her waiting after demanding her immediate attendance. She'd never been the kind of mother who would actually turn up at the airport to greet her plane or make any kind of fuss. 'It's lovely sitting here in the kitchen. I needed a chance to catch my breath and I am so hungry.'

That earned her a big smile from the housekeeper. 'Then eat up, and enjoy. There is plenty more.'

The risotto was pure heaven, creamy and smooth with just the right amount of bite, and Tina took her time to savour it.

'What happened to the gardens, Carmela?' she asked

when she had satisfied her appetite and sat cradling a fragrant espresso. 'It looks so sad.'

The housekeeper nodded and slipped onto one of the stools herself, her hands cupping her own tiny cup. 'The *signora* could no longer afford to pay salaries. She had to let the gardener go, and then her secretary left. I try to keep up the herb garden and some pots, but it is not easy.'

Tina could believe it. 'But she's paying you?'

'She is, when she can. She has promised she will make up any shortfall.'

'Oh, Carmela, that's so wrong. Why have you stayed? Surely you could get a job in any house in Venice?'

'And leave your mother to her own devices?' The older woman drained the last of her coffee and patted her on the hand as she rose to collect the cups and plates. She shrugged. 'My needs are not great. I have a roof over my head and enough to get by. And one day, who knows, maybe your mother's fortunes will change.'

'How? Does it look like she'll marry again?'

Carmela simply smiled, too loyal to comment. Everyone who knew Lily knew that every one of her marriages after her first had been a calculated exercise in wealth accumulation, even if her plans had come unstuck with Eduardo. 'I meant now that you are here.'

Tina was about to reply that she doubted there was anything she could do when she heard footsteps on the tiles and her mother's voice growing louder… 'Carmela, I thought I heard voices—' She appeared at the door. 'Oh, Valentina, I see you've arrived. I was just speaking to your father. I would have told him you were here if I'd known.'

Tina slipped from her stool, feeling the warmth from the kitchen leach away in the uncomfortable assessment she gauged in her mother's eyes. 'Hello, Lily,' she said, cursing herself for the way she always felt inadequate in her mother's presence. 'Did Dad call to talk to me?'

'Not really,' she said vaguely. 'We just had some… business…to discuss. Nothing to worry about,' her mother assured her, as she air-kissed her daughter's cheeks and whirled away again with barely a touch, leaving just a waft of her own secret Chanel blend that one of her husbands had commissioned for her in her wake. Lily had always loved the classics. Labels and brand names, the more exclusive the better. And as she took in her mother's superbly fitted silk dress and Louboutin heels, clearly nothing had changed. The garden might be shabby, but there was nothing shabby about her mother's appearance. She looked as glamorous as ever.

'You look tired,' Lily said frankly, her gaze not stopping at her eyes as she took in her day-old tank top and faded jeans and clearly found them wanting as she accepted a cup of tea from Carmela. 'You might want to freshen up and find something nicer to wear before we go out.'

Tina frowned. 'Go out?' What she really wanted was a shower and twelve hours sleep. But if her mother had lined up an appointment with her bank, then maybe it was worth making a head start on her problems. 'What did you have in mind?'

'I thought we could go shopping. There's some lovely new boutiques down on the Calle Larga 22 Marzo. I thought it would be fun to take my grown-up daughter out shopping.'

'Shopping?' Tina regarded her mother with disbelief. 'You really want to go shopping?'

'Is there a problem with that?'

'What are you planning on spending? Air?'

Her mother laughed. 'Oh, don't be like that, Valentina.

Can't we celebrate you being back in Venice with a new outfit or two?'

'I'm serious, Lily. You asked me to come—no, scrub that, you *demanded* I come—because you said you are about to be thrown out of this place, and the minute I get here you expect to go shopping. I don't get it.'

'Valentina—'

'No! I left Dad up to his neck in problems so I could come and sort yours out, like you asked me to.'

Lily looked to Carmela for support but the housekeeper had found a spot on her stove top that required serious cleaning. She turned back to her daughter, her voice held together with a thin steel thread.

'Well, in that case—'

'In that case, maybe we should get started.' And then, because her mother looked stunned, and because she knew she was tired and jet-lagged and less tolerant than usual of her mother's excesses, she sighed. 'Look, Lily, maybe once we get everything sorted out—maybe then there'll be time for shopping. I tell you what, why don't you get all the paperwork ready, and I'll come and have a look as soon as I've showered and changed? Maybe it's nowhere near as bad as you think.'

An hour later, Tina buried her head in her hands and wished herself back on the family farm working sixteen-hour days. Wished herself anywhere that wasn't here, facing up to the nightmare that was her mother's accounts.

For a moment she considered going through the documents again, just one more time, just to check she wasn't wrong, that she hadn't miscalculated and overestimated the extent of her mother's debt, but she'd been through everything twice already now. Been through endless bank and credit card statements. Pored over loan document after loan document, all the time struggling with a dictionary alongside to make sense of the complex legal terms written in a language not her first.

She had made no mistake.

She rubbed the bridge of her nose and sighed. From the very start, when she'd seen the mass of paperwork her mother kept hidden away in an ancient ship's chest—almost as if she'd convinced herself that out of sight really was out of mind—the signs had been ominous, but she'd kept hope alive as she'd worked to organise and sort the mess into some kind of order—hope that somewhere amidst it all would be the key to rescuing her mother from financial ruin.

She was no accountant, it was true, but doing the farm's meagre accounts had meant she'd had to learn the hard way about balancing books, and as she'd slowly pieced the puzzle together, it was clear that there was no key, just as there would be no rescue.

Her mother's outgoings were ten times what was being earned on the small estate Eduardo had left her, and Luca Barbarigo was apparently happily funding the difference.

But where was Lily spending all the money when she was no longer paying salaries? She'd sorted through and found a handful of accounts from the local grocer, another batch from a clutch of boutiques and while her mother hadn't stinted on her own wardrobe, there was nowhere near enough to put her this deep into financial trouble. *Unless...*

She looked around the room, the space so cluttered with ornaments that they seemed to suck up the very oxygen. Next to her desk a lamp burned, but not just any lamp. This was a tree, with a gnarled twisted trunk that sprouted two dozen pink flowers and topped with a dozen curved branches fringed with green leaves that ended in more pink flowers but this time boasting light globes, and the entire thing made of glass.

It was hideous.

And that was only one of several lamps, she realised, dotted around the corners of the room and perched over chairs like triffids.

Were they new?

The chandelier she remembered because it was such a fantastical confection of yellow daffodils, pink peonies and some blue flower she had never been able to put a name to, and all set amidst a flurry of cascading ivory glass stems. There was no way she could have forgotten that, and she was sure she would have remembered the lamps if they had been here the last time she had visited.

Likewise, the fish bowls dotted around the room on every available flat surface. There was even one parked on the corner of the desk where she was working. She'd actually believed it was a fish bowl at first, complete with goldfish and bubbles and coral, rocks and weed. Until she'd looked up ten minutes into her work and realised the goldfish hadn't moved. Nothing had moved, because it was solid glass.

They were all solid glass.

Oh God. She rested her head on the heel of one hand. Surely this wasn't where her mother's funds had disappeared?

'Are you tired, Valentina?' asked Lily, edging into the room, picking up one glass ornament after another in the cluttered room, polishing away some nonexistent speck of dust before moving on. 'Should I call Carmela to bring more coffee?'

Tina shook her head as she sat back in her chair. No amount of coffee was going to fix this problem. Because it wasn't tiredness she was feeling right now. It was utter—*downright*—despair.

And a horrible sinking feeling that she knew where the money had all gone…

'What are all these amounts in the bank statements, Lily? The ones that seem to go out every month—there are no invoices that I can find to match them.'

Lily shrugged. 'Just household expenses. This and that. You know how it is.'

'No. I need you to tell me how it is. What kind of household expenses?'

'Just things for the house! I'm allowed to buy things for the house, aren't I?'

'Not if it's bankrupting you in the process! Where is the money going, Lily? Why is there no record of it?'

'Oh—' she tried to laugh, flapping her hands around as if Tina's questions were nothing but nuisance value '—I don't bother with the details. Luca keeps track of all that. His cousin owns the factory.'

'What factory? The glass factory, Lily? Is that where all your money is going as quickly as Luca Barbarigo tops you up? You're spending it all on glass?'

'It's not like that!'

'No?'

'No! Because he gives me a twenty per cent discount, so I'm not paying full price for anything. I've saved a fortune.'

Tina surveyed her mother with disbelief. So very beautiful and so very stupid. 'So every time you get a loan top-up from Luca Barbarigo, you go shopping at his cousin's factory.'

Her mother had the sheer audacity to shrug. Tina wanted to shake her. 'He sends a water taxi. It doesn't cost me a thing.'

'No, Lily,' she said, pushing back her chair to stand.

There was no point in searching for an answer any longer. Not when there wasn't one. 'It's cost you everything! I just don't believe how you could be so selfish. Carmela is working down there for a pittance you sometimes neglect to pay. You can barely afford to pay her, and yet you fill up this crumbling palazzo with so much weight of useless glass, it's a wonder it hasn't collapsed into the canal under the weight of it all!'

'Carmela gets her board!'

'While you get deeper and deeper into debt! What will happen to her, do you think, when Luca Barbarigo throws you both out on the street? Who will look after her then?'

Her mother blinked, her lips tightly pursed, and for a moment Tina thought she almost looked vulnerable.

'You won't let that happen, will you?' she said meekly. 'You'll talk to him?'

'For all the good it will do, yes, I'll talk to him. But I don't see why it will make a shred of difference. He's got you so tightly stitched up financially, why should he relax the stranglehold now?'

'Because he's Eduardo's nephew.'

'So?'

'And Eduardo loved me.'

Indulged you, more like it, Tina thought, cursing the stupid pride of the man for letting his wife think his fortune was bottomless and not bothering to curb her spending while he was alive, and not caring what might happen to his estate when he was gone.

'Besides,' her mother continued, 'you'll make him see reason. He'll listen to you.'

'I doubt it.'

'But you were friends—'

'We were never friends! And if you knew the things he said about you, you would know he was never your friend either, no matter how much money he is so happy to lend you.'

'What did he say? Tell me!'

Tina shook her head. She'd said too much. She didn't want to remember the ugly things he'd said before she'd slapped his smug face. Instead she pulled her jacket from the back of her chair. 'I'm sorry, Lily. I need to get some fresh air.'

'Valentina!'

She fled the veritable glass museum with the sound of her mother's voice still ringing in her ears, running down the marble steps and out past the five-hundred-year-old well with no idea where she was going, simply that she had to get away.

Away from the lamps that looked like trees and the goldfish frozen in glass and the tons of chandeliers that threatened to sink the building under their weight.

Ran from her mother's sheer naivety and her unbelievable inability to read the terms of an agreement and then to blithely disregard them as unimportant when she did.

Fleeing from her own fear that there was no way she could sort out her mother's problems and be home in a mere three days. Her mother was drowning in debt, just as the ancient palazzo itself was threatening to collapse into the canal and drown under the weight of tons of expensive but ultimately useless glass.

And there was not one thing she could do about it. This trip was a complete waste of time and money. It was pointless. There was nothing she could do.

She turned left out of the gate, heading back down the narrow *calle* towards the canal and a vaporetto that would take her somewhere—anywhere—her mother was not. And at the next corner she turned tight left again, too suddenly to see anyone coming, too consumed with her thoughts to remember she should be walking on the other side of the path. And much too suddenly to stop until his big hands were at her shoulders, braking her before she could collide headlong into his chest, punching the air from her lungs in the process. Air that had already conveyed the unmistakable news to her brain.

Luca.

CHAPTER FOUR

HIS eyes were shuttered behind dark glasses, and still she caught a glint of something behind the lenses as he recognised her, some flash of recognition that was mirrored in the upwards tweak of his lips, and she hated him all the more for it. Just as she hated the sizzle where his long fingers burned into her skin.

'Valentina?' he said, in a voice that must have been a gift from the gods at his birth, stroking like a pure dark velvet assault on her senses. 'Is it you?'

She tugged fruitlessly against his steel grip to be free. He was too close, so close that the air was flavoured with the very essence of him, one hundred per cent male with just a hint of Bulgari, a scent that worked to lure her closer even as she struggled to keep her distance. A scent that was like a key opening up the lid on memories she'd rather forget and sending fragments from the past hurtling through her brain, fragments that contained the memory of that scent—of taking his nipple between her teeth and breathing him in; of the rasp of his whiskered chin against her throat making her gasp; and the feel of him driving into her with the taste of his name in her mouth.

And she cursed the combination of a velvet voice and an evocative scent; cursed that she remembered in way too much detail and the fact that he still looked as good as he always had and hadn't put on twenty kilos and lost his hair since she had last seen him.

Cursed the fact that there was clearly no justice in this world.

For instead he was as beautiful as she remembered, a linen jacket over a white shirt that clung to his lean muscled chest as if it were a second skin, and camel-coloured linen trousers bound low over his hips by a wide leather belt.

He looked every bit the urbane Italian male, as polished and sleek as the streamlined water taxis that prowled the canals, the powerful aristocrats of this watery world. And she was suddenly aware of the disparity between them, with her raw-faced from her shower and dressed in faded jeans and a chain-store jade-coloured vest that was perfectly at home on the farm or even in town but here and now in his presence felt tired and cheap.

'But of course it is you. My apologies, I almost didn't recognise you with your clothes on.'

And a velvet voice turned to sandpaper, to scrape across senses already reeling from the shock of their meeting and leaving them raw and stinging.

'Luca,' she managed in an ice-laden voice designed to slice straight through his smugness, 'I'd like to say it's good to see you again, but right now I just want you to let me go.'

His smile only widened, but he did let her go then, even if his hands lingered at her shoulders just a fraction longer than necessary, the shudder as his thumbs swept an arc across her skin as they departed and left her shivery just as unwelcome. 'Where are you off to in such a hurry? I understood you had only now arrived.'

There was no point being surprised or asking how he knew. Her mother had been making calls when she'd arrived. One of them was to her father, her mother had said, but was another to Luca Barbarigo, sorting out the next instalment of her loan so she could purchase a new barge-ful of glassware? She wouldn't be surprised. For all her mother's protests about the unfair actions of the man, she needed him for her supply of funds like a drug addict needed their supply of crack cocaine. She didn't waste time being polite. 'What's it to you where I am going?'

'Only that I might have missed you. I was coming to pay my respects.'

'Why? So you could gloat to my face about my mother's pathetic money management skills? Don't bother, I've known about them for ever. It's hardly news to me. I'm sorry you've wasted your time but I'll be heading back to Australia the first flight I can get. And now, if you'll excuse me…' She made to move past him but it wasn't easy. In the busy *calle* he was too tall, too broad across the shoulders. His very presence seemed to absorb what little space there was. But as soon as this next group of tourists passed…

He shifted to the right, blocking her escape. 'You're leaving Venice so soon?'

She tried to ignore what his presence was doing to her blood pressure. Tried to pretend it was anger with her mother that was setting her skin to burn and her senses to overload. 'What would be the point of staying? I'm sure you're not as naive as my mother, Signore Barbarigo. You must know there is nothing I can do to save her from financial ruin. Not after the way you've so neatly stitched her up.'

His eyes glinted in the thin light, and Tina had no doubt the heated spark came not from what was left of the sun, but from a place deep inside.

'So combatative, Valentina? Surely we can talk like reasonable people.'

'But that would require you to be a reasonable person, Signore Barbarigo and, having met you in the past, and having examined my mother's accounts, I would hazard the opinion that you have not one reasonable bone in your body.'

He laughed out loud, a sound that reverberated between the brick walls and bounced all the way up to the fading sky, grinding on her senses. 'Perhaps you are right, Valentina. But that does not stop your mother from believing that you will rescue her from the brink of ruin.'

'Then she is more of a fool than I thought. You have no intention of letting her off the hook, do you? You won't be happy until you have thrown her out of the palazzo!'

Heads turned in their direction, ears of passing tourists pricking up at her raised voice, eager to happen upon a possible conflict to add colour and local spice to their Venetian experience.

'Please, Valentina,' he said, pushing her back towards the wall and leaning in close, as if they were having no more than a lovers' tiff. 'Do you wish to discuss your mother's financial affairs in a public street as if it is fodder for so many tourists' ears? What will they think of us Venetians? That we are not civilised enough to conduct our affairs in private?'

Once again he was too close—so close that she could feel his warm breath fanning her face—too close to be able to ignore his scent or not feel the heat emanating from his firm chest or to be able to think rationally, other than to rebut the obvious.

'I am no Venetian.'

'No. You are Australian and very forthright. I admire that in you. But now, perhaps it is time to take this conversation somewhere more private.' He indicated back in the direction she had come. 'Please. We can discuss this in your mother's house. Or, if you prefer, you can come with me to mine. I assure you, it is only a short walk.'

And meet him on his territory? No way in the world. She might have been trying to escape her mother's house, but it was still the lesser of two evils. Besides, if there were going to be some home truths flying around, maybe it was better her mother was there to hear them. 'Then the palazzo. But only because I have a few more things I want to tell you before I leave.'

'I can hardly wait,' she heard him mutter as she wheeled around and headed back in the direction she had come. So smug, she thought, wishing there was something she could do or say to wipe the expression from his face. Was he so sure of Lily's hopelessness that he had known her trip here was futile from the start? Was he laughing at her—at the pointlessness of it all?

She almost growled as she headed back down the *calle*, her senses prickling with the knowledge he was right behind her, prickling with the sensation of his eyes burning into her back. She had to fight the impulse to turn and stare him down but then he would know that she felt his heated gaze and his smugness would escalate from unbearable to insufferable, so she kept her eyes rigidly ahead and tried to pretend she didn't care.

Carmela met them at the palazzo door, smiling uncertainly as she looked from one to the other. But then Luca smiled and turned on the charm as he greeted her in their own language and even though Carmela knew that her future in this place was held by little more than a gossamer thread this man could sever at any time, Tina would swear the older woman actually blushed. She hated him all the more for it in that moment, hated him for this power to make women melt under the sheer onslaught of his smile.

'Your mother has taken to her bed,' Carmela said, apologising for her absence. 'She said she has a headache.'

Luca arched an eyebrow in Tina's direction. She ignored him as Carmela showed them upstairs to the main reception room, promising to bring coffee and refreshments. It was a massive room with high ceilings and pastel-decorated walls that should have been airy and bright but was rendered small by the countless cabinets and tables piled high with glass ornaments, figurines and crystal goblets and lamps of every shape and description, glass that now glinted ruby-red as the setting sunlight streamed in through the wide four-door windows.

It was almost pretty, she thought, a glittering world of glass and illusion, if you could forget about what it had cost.

'You've lost weight, Valentina,' came his voice behind her. 'You've been working too hard.'

And it rankled with her that all the time he'd been following her he'd been sizing her up. Comparing her to how she'd been three years ago and finding her wanting. No doubt comparing her to all his other women and finding her wanting. *Damn it, she didn't want to think about his other women! They were welcome to him.* She spun around. 'We've all changed, Luca. We're all a few years older. Hopefully a bit wiser into the deal. I know I am.'

He smiled and picked up a paperweight that glowed red from a collection from a side table, resting it in the palm of his big hand. 'Some things I see haven't changed. You are still as beautiful as ever, Valentina.' He smiled and examined the glass in his hand before replacing it with the others and moving on, finding a slow path around the cluttered room and around her, pausing to examine a tiny crystal animal here, a gilt-edged glass plate there, touching just a fingertip to it before looking up at her again. 'Perhaps, you are a little more prickly than I remember. Perhaps there is a little more spice. But then I recall you were always very...*passionate*.'

He lingered over the word as if he were donning that velvet glove to stroke her memories and warm her senses. She swallowed, fighting back the tide of the past and a surge of heat low in her belly. 'I don't want to hear it,' she said, turning on the spot as he continued to circle the room, touching a hand to the head of a glass boy holding a lantern aloft as if the golden-skinned child was real and not just another of her mother's follies. 'Instead, I want to tell you that I know what you're doing.'

He tilted his head. 'And what, exactly, am I doing?'

'I've been through Lily's accounts. You keep lending her money, advance after advance. Money that she turns straight around to purchase more of this—' she waved her hand around the room '—from your own cousin's glass factory on Murano.'

He shrugged. 'What can I say? I am a banker. Lending people money is an occupational hazard. But surely it is not my responsibility how they see fit to use those funds.'

'But you know she has no income to speak of to pay you back, and still you loan her more.'

He smiled and held up his index finger. 'Ah. But income is only one consideration a banker must take into account when evaluating a loan risk. You are forgetting that your mother has, what we call in the business, exceptional assets.'

She snorted. 'You've noticed her assets then.' The words were out before she could snatch them back, and now they hung in the space like crystal drops from a chandelier, heavy and fat and waiting to be inspected in the light.

He raised an eyebrow in question. 'I was talking about the palazzo.'

'So was I,' she said, too quickly. 'I don't know what you're thinking about.'

He laughed a little and ran the tips of his fingers across the rim of a fluted glass bowl on a mantelpiece as he passed, continuing his circuit of the room. Such long fingers, she couldn't help but notice, such a feather-light touch. A touch she remembered on her skin. A touch she had thought about so often in the dark of night when sleep had eluded her and she had felt so painfully alone.

'Your mother is a very beautiful woman, Valentina. Does it bother you that I might notice?'

She blinked, trying to get a grip back on the conversation, tilting her head higher as he came closer. 'Why should it?'

'I don't know. Unless you're worried that I have slept with Lily. That maybe I am sleeping with her?' He stopped before her and smiled. 'Does that bother you, *cara*?'

'I don't want to know! I don't care! It's no business of mine who you sleep with.'

'Of course not. And, of course, she is a very beautiful woman.'

'So you said.' The words were ground out through her teeth.

'Although nowhere—*nowhere*—near as beautiful as her daughter.'

He touched those fingers to her brow, smoothing back a wayward strand of hair. She gasped, shivering at the touch, thinking she should stop him—that she should step away—when in truth she could feel herself leaning closer.

It was Luca who stepped away, dropping his hand, and she blinked, a little stunned, feeling as if she had conceded a point to him, knowing that she had to regain the high ground.

'You told my mother we were old friends.'

He shrugged and sat down on a red velvet armchair, his long legs lazily sprawled out wide, his elbows resting on the arms. 'Aren't we?'

'We were never friends.'

'Come now, Valentina.' Something about the way he said her name seemed almost as if he were stroking her again with that velvet glove and she crossed her arms over her chest to hide an instinctive and unwanted reaction. 'Surely, given what we have shared…'

'We shared nothing! We spent one night together, one night that I have regretted ever since.' *And not only because of the things you said and the way we parted.*

'I don't remember it being quite so unpleasant.'

'Perhaps you recall another night. Another woman. I'm sure there have been so many, it must get quite confusing. But I'm not confused. You are no friend of mine. You are nothing to me. You never were, and you never will be.'

She thought he might leave then. She was hoping he might realise they had nothing more to say to each other and just go. But while he pulled his long legs in and sat up higher in the chair, he did not get up. His eyes lost all hint of laughter and took on a focus—a hard-edged gleam—that, coupled with his pose, with his legs poised like springs beneath him, felt almost predatory. If she turned and ran, she thought, even if there was a way to run in this cluttered showroom, he would be out of his chair and upon her in a heartbeat. Her own heart kicked up a notch, tripping inside her chest like a frightened gazelle.

'When your mother first came to me for a loan,' he said in a voice that dared her not to pay attention to each and every syllable, 'I was going to turn her down. I had no intention of lending her the money.'

She didn't say anything. She sensed there was no point in asking him what had changed his mind—that he intended telling her anyway—even if she didn't want to know. On some very primal level, she recognised that she did not want to know, that, whatever it was, she was not going to want to hear this.

'I should see about that coffee—' she said, making a move for the stairs.

'No,' he said, standing and barring her exit in one fluid movement, leaving her wondering how such a big man could move with such economy and grace. 'Coffee can wait until I've finished. Until you've heard this.'

She looked up at him, at the angles and planes of his face that were both so beautiful and so cruel, looked at the place where a tiny crease betrayed a rarely seen dimple in his cheek, studied the shallow cleft in his chin, and she wondered that she remembered every part of him so vividly and in such detail, that nothing of his features came as a surprise but more as a vindication of her memory.

And only then she realised he was studying her just as intently, just as studiously, and she turned her eyes away. *Because she had stared at him too long*, she told herself, *not because she was worried what he might be remembering about her.*

'I didn't have to lend that money to your mother,' he continued. 'But then I remembered one long night in a room warmed by an open fire, with sheepskin rugs on the floor and a feather quilt to warm the wide bed. And I remembered a woman with skin the colour of cream with amber eyes and golden hair and who left too angry and much too soon.'

She glared at him, clamping her fists and her thighs and

refusing to let his words bury themselves in the places they wanted to go. 'You lent my mother money to get back at me? Because I slapped you? You really are mad!'

'You're right. I can't give you all the credit. Because in lending your mother money, I saw the opportunity to take back Eduardo's home—this palazzo—before it collapsed into the canal from neglect. I owed Eduardo that, even if I wanted nothing to do with his wife. But that wasn't the only reason. I also wanted to give you a second chance.'

'To slap you again? You make it sound so tempting.' Right now her curling fist ached to lash out at something. Why not his smug face?

He laughed at that. 'Some say a banker's life must be dull: days filled with endless meetings and boring conversations about corporate finance and interest rate margins. But it doesn't have to be like that. Sometimes it can be much more rewarding.'

'By dreaming up fantasies? Look, I don't care how you while away your hours—I really don't want to know—just leave me out of them.'

'Then you are more selfish than I thought—' his voice turned serious '—your mother is in serious financial trouble. She could lose the palazzo. In fact she *will* lose the palazzo. Don't you care that your mother could be homeless?'

'That will be on your head, not on mine. I'm not the one threatening to throw her out.'

'And yet you could still save her.'

'How? I don't have access to the kind of funds my mother owes you, even if I did want to help.'

'Who said anything about wanting your money?'

There was a chilling note to his delivery, as if she should indeed know exactly what kind of currency he was considering. But no, surely he could not mean *that*?

'I have nothing that would interest any banker and convince them to forgive a debt.'

'You underestimate yourself, *cara*. You have something that might encourage this banker to forgive your mother's debt.'

She shook her head. 'I don't think so!'

'Listen to what I offer, Valentina. I am not a beast, whatever you may think. I do not want your mother to suffer the indignity of being thrown out of her home. Indeed, I have an apartment overlooking the Grand Canal ready and waiting for your mother to move into. She will own it free of any encumbrance and she will draw a monthly pension. All that stands in the way is you.' He smiled, the smile of a crocodile, the predator back in residence under his skin.

Her own skin prickled with both suspicion and fascination. He was a beautiful specimen of a man. He always had been. But she'd known the man, she'd known what he was capable of, and her self-protection senses were on high alert. 'And are you going to tell me what I have to do in order to win this happy ever after for my mother?'

'Nothing I know you will not enjoy. I simply require you to share my bed.'

She blinked, expecting to wake up at any moment. For surely she was so jet-lagged that she'd fallen asleep on her feet and was busy dreaming a fantasy. No, not a fantasy. *A nightmare.* 'As simple as that?' she echoed. 'You're saying that you will let my mother off the hook, you will gift her an apartment in which to live and pay her an allowance, and all I have to do is sleep with you?'

'I told you it was simple.'

Did he imagine she was? Did he not realise what he was asking her? To sell herself to him like some kind of whore—and all to save her mother? 'Thank you for coming, Signore Barbarigo. I'm sure you don't have to trouble Carmela to find your way out. I'm sure you can find the way.'

'Valentina, do you know what you are saying no to?'

'Some kind of paradise, apparently, the way you make it sound. Except I'm not in the market. I'm not looking for paradise. I certainly wouldn't expect to find it in your bed.'

'You might want to reconsider your options. I do not think you are giving this offer the serious consideration it deserves.'

'And I don't think you're giving me any credit for knowing when I've heard enough.'

'And your mother? You care not for what happens to her?'

'My mother is a big girl, Mr Barbarigo. She got herself into this mess, she can damned well get herself out of it.'

'And if that means she loses the palazzo and ends up homeless?'

'Then so be it. She'll just have to find somewhere else to live, like anyone else who overspends their budget.'

'I'm surprised at you. Her own daughter, and you will do nothing to help her.'

'You overplayed your hand, Luca, imagining I even cared. I will play no part in your sordid game. Throw my mother out if you must. Maybe then she might learn her lesson. But don't expect me to prostitute myself to bail her out. When I said what we had was over, I meant it.'

He nodded then, and she felt a rush of relief like she had never known before. She had just consigned her mother to her fate, it was true, but it was no worse a result than she had come here half expecting. Perhaps if her mother had been more of a mother, one who inspired loyalty and affection, she might even consider Luca's barbaric bargain. For five minutes at least. Then again, a mother like that would never put her in a position such as this. A mother like that would never have fallen victim to such an opportunistic despot.

'In that case you give me no choice. I will go. And I will call your father and let him know the bad news.'

'My father?' she asked, with an ice-cold band of fear tightening around her chest. Lily had been talking to her father on the phone when she'd arrived and she'd never got around to finding out exactly why, even though it had seemed odd. What had they cooked up between themselves? 'Why would you call him? What's Mitch got to do with this?'

'Does it matter? I thought you wanted no more part of this.'

'If it's about my father, then of course it concerns me. Why would you need to call him?'

'Because Lily spoke to him today.'

'I know that,' she snapped, impatient. 'And?'

'And he didn't want to see your trip wasted. Lily told me he would do anything for you, and apparently she was right. He offered to put up the farm as security if you could not find a way to help.'

CHAPTER FIVE

'I CAN'T believe you dragged my father into this!' Tina burst into her mother's room, livid. There was no risk of waking her, she'd just ordered Carmela to bring her brandy. 'What the hell were you thinking?'

Luca had departed, taking his smug expression with him but leaving a poisoned atmosphere in his wake and now Lily wasn't the only one with a headache. Tina's temples pounded with a message of war.

'What are you doing in here? What's all this screaming?'

Tina swiped open the curtains in the dark room, letting in what little light remained of the day. Too little light. She snapped on a switch and was rewarded by a veritable vineyard lighting up above her mother's bed head, clusters of grapes in autumn colours, russets and pinks and golds, dangling from the ceiling amid wafer-thin 'leaves' of green and pink. For a moment she was too blindsided to speak.

'What the hell is that?' she demanded when at last she'd found her tongue.

'You don't like it?' her mother said, sitting up, looking up at the lights, sounding surprised.

'It's hideous. Just like everything else in this glass mausoleum.'

'Valentina, do you have to be so rude? I'll have you know I don't buy things to please you.'

'Clearly. But right now I'm more concerned about whatever it was you got Dad to agree to. Luca said he'd put the farm on the line. For you. To bail you out. If I couldn't find a way.'

'You saw Luca?' Lily scambled from the bed, pulled on a rose-pink silk robe that wafted around her slim body as it settled. 'When? Is he still here?'

'He's gone and good riddance to him. But not before he put his seedy deal on the table. Were you in on it, mother dearest? Was it you who came up with the idea of swapping your daughter for your debt?'

Lily blinked up at her. 'He said that?' And her mother looked so stunned Tina knew there was no way she could have been in on it. 'That does explain a few things, I suppose. Well, aren't you the lucky one. And I thought he wasn't interested in sex.'

'You didn't! Oh, please God, tell me you didn't proposition him.'

She shrugged, sitting at a table, picking up a cloth in one hand, a glass dolphin in the other, absently rubbing its head. 'Turning fifty is no joy, Valentina, you mark my words. Nobody wants you. Nobody sees you. You might just as well be invisible when it comes to men.'

'There's nothing flattering about being asked to be someone's mistress, Lily!'

'But of course there is. He's a very good-looking man.' And then she stopped rubbing and stared into the middle distance as if she was building an entire story around the possibilities. 'Just think, if you play your cards right, he might even marry you…'

'I told him I wouldn't do it.'

Her mother looked at her, and Tina saw an entire fantasy crashing down in her eyes. 'Oh.'

'And that's when he told me about Dad, and agreeing to put up the farm. Is that why you were on the phone to him, Lily? Looking for a Plan B in case I couldn't save you? Begging for favours from a man you abandoned with a baby more than twenty-five years ago? A man who by rights should hate your guts.'

'He doesn't, though. I think Mitchell was the only man who ever really loved me.'

'Well, you sure made a mess of that.'

'I still don't understand what your problem is. People would kill to sleep with Luca Barbarigo.'

And the desire to shock her mother just for once, instead of being the one who was always shocked, was too great. 'That's just it. I *have* slept with him.'

'You sly girl,' she said, swapping the dolphin for another, this one with a baby swimming alongside. 'And you never let on? So why make such a big deal out of it now?'

And that simple question told her more about her mother than she ever wanted to know. 'It ended badly.'

'Because he didn't express his undying love for you? Oh God, Valentina, you're so naive sometimes.'

Her mother's words stung, deep inside where she'd promised she'd never hurt again. And maybe that was why she said it. Because she didn't want to be the only one hurting here. 'He said I was a chip off the old block. That, like you, I did my best work on my back!'

Her mother paused, forgetting momentarily about the delicate glass dolphin in her lap that she'd been lovingly dusting till then. And then she laughed, absolutely delighted. 'He said that? And you didn't take it as a compliment?' She took one look at her daughter's stricken face. 'You didn't, did you?' She shrugged and started polishing again, before she gave it a final check in the light and replaced it with another ornament. Rub rub rub. Polish polish polish. And the more she polished, the more Tina's nerves screamed.

'Would you please stop doing that?'

'Doing what?'

'Dusting those wretched ornaments of yours.'

'Valentina,' her mother said, incensed, rubbing on, 'they're Murano glass, they deserve to be shown to best advantage. Of course I have to dust them.'

'I was pregnant, you know!'

Lily looked up at her, and this time she put the ornament right back on the side table where it had come from. Finally, Tina thought. Finally she managed to look aghast. 'You were pregnant? To Luca Barbarigo?'

Tina nodded, a sudden tightness in her throat, a sudden and unbidden urge to cry stinging her eyes as she released a secret she had been holding inside for too long. Finally her mother might understand.

Finally.

Lily just sat there and shook her head. 'So why didn't you make him marry you?'

'What?'

'Don't you know how rich he is? His family were once Doges of Venice. He's Venetian nobility and you didn't marry him?'

'Lily, we had a one-night stand. One night. A baby wasn't part of the deal. Anyway, I lost the baby. And thank you so much for asking about the fate of your grandchild!'

'But if you'd married him,' her mother continued, unabashed, 'then we wouldn't be in this mess now.'

Tina's world reeled and spun. 'Didn't you hear me? I lost the baby. At twenty weeks. Do you have any idea what that's like, giving birth to a child that is destined to die?'

Lily flicked away the argument as if it were no more than a speck of dust on one of her ornaments. 'You didn't really want a child, did you? Besides, you could have been married by then. You would have been, if you'd told me at the time. I would have arranged your marriage within a week.'

'And what if I didn't want to get married?'

'That's hardly the point. You should have made him do the honourable thing.'

Tina doubted she had ever hated her mother quite so much. 'Like you made Mitch do when you got pregnant? Tell me, Lily, were you hoping for a miscarriage once you had that ring on your finger? Were you hoping to escape the birth once you had the husband, given you never really wanted a child?'

'That's not fair!'

'Isn't it? Sorry I didn't oblige. Lucky, though, in a way, given the mess you're in now.'

She turned to leave. 'Goodbye, Lily. I don't expect to see you again while I'm here.'

'Where are you going?'

And she looked back over her shoulder. 'To hell. But don't go thinking it's on your account.'

The taxi dropped him back at the water door of his own palazzo overlooking the Grand Canal. Aldo came down to meet him, swinging open the iron gate as he alighted from the vessel. 'And the company you were expecting?'

'A change of plan, Aldo. I will be dining alone tonight. I will eat in the study.'

Luca crossed the tiled floor and took the marble steps up into the house three at a time. A temporary change of plan, he had no doubt. Once Valentina slept on the choices she had, she would see she had no choice at all. She would soon come crawling, begging for him to rescue her family from the nightmare of her mother's making.

He entered the study, but eschewed the wide desk where his computer and work waited patiently and went straight to the windows instead, opening a window door leading to a balcony and gazing out over the canal at night, the vaporettos lit up with the flash of a hundred cameras, the heavy barges that performed the grunt work in place of trucks. Never did he tire of the endless tapestry of life in Venice, the slap of water against the pilings, the rich tenor strains of a gondolier as he massaged his gondola's way along the canals. But then his family had been here for centuries after all. No wonder he sometimes felt his veins ran not with blood but with water from these very canals.

It spoke to him now. Told him to be patient. That he was closer than he thought.

He saw the colour of her eyes in the golden light from a window across the canal. Amber eyes and hair shot with golden lights—she might have lost weight, she might have been travelling for more than a day and the skin under her eyes tired, but the intervening years had been good to her. She was more beautiful than he remembered.

And he hungered for her.

But she would soon come crawling.

And he would have her.

She got the address from Carmela, who hugged her tight to her chest before putting her at arm's length and kissing her solemnly on both cheeks. 'You come back if you need anything, anything at all. You come back and see Carmela. I will help you, *bella*.'

She hugged the older woman back, clutching the piece of paper with the address and the rough map Carmela had drawn for her. Luca had said it wasn't far. It didn't help that evening had closed in and that the canals were inky-black ribbons running between islands of jam-packed buildings, it didn't help that she knew she had been awake for a dozen hours too many to feel alive, but she was running on anger now, her veins infused with one hundred per cent fury, and there was no way she was staying in her mother's house a moment longer and no way she could have slept if she tried.

She made a mistake with the vaporetto, boarding the wrong one in her rush to get away and she had to get off at the next stop and backtrack to find another. She found herself lost in the dark *calles* three times, stumbling onwards as if she were blind until she found a sign on a wall with a name she recognised, telling her she was on the right track.

But all of these inconveniences just gave her the time to think. To reconsider why she was so prepared to jump into the lion's den—a place she had promised herself never to go again.

It wasn't for her mother, she knew. She'd been prepared to turn her back and walk away and leave her mother to her own devices.

It wasn't for herself. Oh God, no. She hated him after what he'd said, and what he'd done. Hated him for not caring when he could have. Hated him for the unsettling, unwanted effect he had on her, even in the midst of hating him. She wanted nothing more to do with the man.

No, this was for her father, who somehow thought that if he helped Lily in this current crisis, he was making it easier on his daughter. What had Lily told him of her plight? What dramas had she woven around the thin ribbons that still bonded them together, even after a divorce of more than twenty years?

But their property was operating on a shoestring, already mortgaged heavily to the banks. Another mortgage, another bad season would see her father's dream ruined.

She could not let him do that, for whatever misguided sense of loyalty he still had.

She could not let it happen.

She made another wrong turn and swore under her breath as she retraced her steps again. But all of the inconveniences of her journey, all these frustrations fed into her anger. So by the time she reached the sign on the locked gate that announced she was at the right number of the right street, she felt ready to tear the gate apart with her bare hands. Instead she pressed a buzzer, waited impatiently the few seconds for a response and asked to see Luca Barbarigo.

When she met with hesitation, she countered it with, 'Tell him it is Tina Henderson...*Valentina* Henderson. He will see me.'

A few moments later the gate clicked open and a stony-faced valet met her at the door, giving her a once-over that told her that in faded jeans and a cheap zip-up jacket she was seriously underdressed for a meeting with his boss. But that was okay because she had plans for her wardrobe. 'Signore Barbarigo will receive you in the study,' he said, before gesturing for her backpack. 'If you would care to leave your bag?'

'I'm good with it,' she said, her hand on the shoulder strap, 'if it's all the same to you.' Luca would be under no misapprehension why she was there if she had anything to do with it. He would know she meant business if she turned up with her pack. Besides, if she was going to be sharing the master's bedchamber, it was going to have to be carried upstairs at some stage.

The valet nodded, his disapproval clear on his set features, and led the way up the wide flight of stairs leading to the noble floor. A stunning palazzo, she registered as they climbed, with terrazzo floors and stuccoed walls and heavy beamed ceilings so high they were in no way oppressive.

Or were they?

Only one flight of steps, but suddenly she needed oxygen, as if the air was thinner the higher they climbed. But it wasn't the air, she knew. It was being here, in the lion's den, about to take on the lion at his own game.

It was anticipation, both terrifying and delicious, for what would come next.

And what could have been a spike of fear and the chance for cowardice to surface and set her fleeing down the stairs turned into a surge of strength. Did he really think she could be forced into something, to tumble meekly into his bed? Damn the man but she would not crawl to him like some simpering virgin begging for favours.

The stairs opened to a sitting room so elegant it could feature in a magazine—maybe the sofas and dark timber leant towards the masculine—but the overall effect was of light and space.

How her mother's house was meant to look, it occurred to her. Probably had looked, before Eduardo had taken her for his wife and she'd become addicted to the factory shops of Murano and let her passion for glass suck up every last euro and every available inch of space.

Through a set of timber doors, the valet led her, and yet another reception room until finally they were at another set of sculpted timber doors where he knocked and showed her in, pulling the door closed behind him as he left.

Her heart kicked up a beat when she saw him.

The lion was in.

He sprawled arrogantly in a chair behind an acre of desk across a room that went on for ever and then some. And still he owned the room. It was an extension of him, paying tribute to his inexorable power. She wrenched her eyes from his and studied the desk before him. Antique if she wasn't mistaken, but masculine and strong and with legs that were solid and built to last whatever the ages would throw at it.

It would do nicely.

'Valentina,' he said, without standing, his voice measured, his dark eyes waiting for answers. 'This is a surprise.'

'Is it?' She looked around at the door. 'Does that lock from the inside?'

He cocked his head, the shadow of a frown pulling his brows closer together. 'Why do you ask?'

She shrugged the straps of her backpack from her shoulders, hoping no hired help was about to rush in—not with what she had planned—before letting the weight drag it to the ground at her feet, making no move to stop it hitting the floor. She summoned up confidence along with a smile she didn't feel. 'It would be a shame to be interrupted.'

'Would it?' he asked, as if he didn't care one way or the other, and she almost panicked and fled while she could. It was so long since she'd last made love. Years since that last unforgettable night with Luca. Was she kidding herself that she could pull this off? She was so unpractised in the arts of the seductress, so unskilled.

And she almost did flee.

Except she noticed the way he'd already eased his body a fraction higher in his seat, his limbs a little less casually positioned.

And so she licked her lips in preparation for the show. Oh God, she was such an amateur! Such a fake! But still she touched a finger to the zip of her jacket and toyed with it a while, teasing it lower—she was way out of her depth and it had to show!—until she was certain he was watching. 'It's warm in here. Don't you think it's warm in here?'

'I can open a window,' he said guardedly, his eyes not leaving her fingers, no part of him looking like it was willing to move far enough to open a window any time soon.

'It's fine,' she said, feeling suddenly empowered, sliding the zip all the slow way down, peeling it from her shoulders lovingly, like a lover would do from behind, sighing a kiss against one bare shoulder. 'It's probably just me.'

'Why are you here?' The words were short, but his trademark velvet voice was thick and already curdling at the edges from heat.

She smiled and flicked off her sandals, cursing when one needed another kick, feeling clumsy. Inadequate for the task. But he wasn't looking at her feet and so she pressed on. 'You offered me a position,' she said, letting him wait for the rest. She tugged the hem of her singlet free from her belted jeans, waited just a moment to ensure she had his full, undivided attention, before pulling it over her head, letting her hair tumble free over her bare shoulders. She put her hands to the belt at her belly, letting her arms frame her breasts, clad in their white T-shirt bra. It was probably the plainest, dullest bra he had ever seen, but right now it was all she had and it was too late to worry about her underwear. Besides, from the glint in Luca's eyes, he probably hadn't even noticed that she was wearing one. That glint gave her the courage she needed if she was going to do this, courage to bare a body nobody had seen for three long years. A body that had been shut away from the world lest it betray her again. Was she asking too much of it now?

She held her breath as she slid the leather of her belt through the buckle and popped the button on her jeans. 'I'm accepting it.'

She slid the zip down, gave a wiggle of her hips to help push them down and hesitated, leaning forward just enough to turn cotton-clad breasts into a cleavage. He wasn't looking relaxed any more, she noticed. He was sitting up. Paying attention. 'Oh. I thought of something,' she said.

'What?' he croaked, his eyes not shifting.

'Conditions.'

Was that a groan she heard or a growl? It didn't matter. Either worked for her. 'Tell me,' he said.

'How long am I supposed to be your mistress? Only you didn't say.'

'I hadn't thought about it. However long it takes.'

'I thought a month.'

'A month?'

'A month would be more than adequate. I mean, I don't know what the going rate for mistresses is, but I'm thinking high end, late model, low mileage—well, that has to be worth more. Right?'

'If you say so.'

'Only I have work to do back home. And I'm sure you have something to be going on with. And it's not like we want this thing messing with our lives, right?'

'Right.'

Her hands lingered at her hips. She looked at him, watching her, feeling the power of his need feeding the anger that had been building ever since that phone call from Lily, the anger that had worked itself into a volcano set to erupt today, and smiled knowingly. *You utter bastard*, she thought with satisfaction. *And you thought you were going to have this all your own way.*

It was almost too good to be true. *Almost.*

'And you will never contact or threaten my father with anything financial or otherwise. Never again.'

'Never.'

It wasn't just too good to be true. It was perfect.

'You have such a lovely big desk, Luca.' She edged her jeans a fraction lower, spun around to give him a view from the back as she eased the soft denim lower, making sure her underwear went with it, and looked at him over her shoulder. 'It would be such a shame to waste all that glorious space on work, don't you think?'

'I think,' he said, standing awkwardly, kicking off his loafers while he attacked the buttons of his own shirt, shrugging it off to expose a chest made in heaven and stolen from the gods. 'I think you need help getting those jeans off.'

CHAPTER SIX

CONTROL. It was one of the things Luca prided himself on. He had patience. He had nerve. He had control of his life and his world. It was the way he liked things to be. It was the way things had to be.

But watching a flaxen haired, amber-eyed minx from Australia strip down to her underwear in his study was threatening to bring him undone.

If only she could get those damned jeans off.

She laughed when he picked her up, the sound half-hysterical, half-intoxicated, wild and free, and he was intoxicated as he spun her around and headed for the desk, sweeping it clear with one arm, sending papers and pencils and phones scattering in all directions before he planted her hard upon the desk and ripped off her jeans, tearing the bra from her breasts with a snap in the next testosterone-fuelled action.

That gave him pause. Naked on his desk, her legs parted by his, she was almost too much to take in with his eyes, too much for one hand to drink in as it swept over creamy skin from knee to thigh to belly to cup one perfect breast.

She stopped laughing then, her breath coming fast and furious, her eyes wide as he pulled his belt free, tugged his zip down and kicked off his pants, her eyes so suddenly cold as he freed his aching erection that she looked almost...*angry*.

'I hate you,' she said, confirming it, her lips tight around the words, baring her sharp white teeth, and that was fine. That was good, because for a moment she'd blindsided him with that impromptu striptease and he'd felt a glimmer of...*something*...that had hovered and curled around uncomfortably in his gut. But hatred he could work with.

Hatred would make her submission all the more satisfying.

And then he would dump her and she could hate him even more.

'Excellent,' he said, slamming open a drawer and rummaging through the contents until he found what he was looking for, shaking a packet free one-handed from the box. He tore it open with his teeth and had it on in record time, spreading her thighs wider to find her centre.

Slick and hot. Oh God.

He calmed himself long enough to stay poised at her entrance, his thumb working at that sensitive nub, watching the hatred in her amber eyes muddy with need, sensing the panting desperation of her breathing. *Oh yes, she hated him all right.*

'I'm so glad we understand each other,' he said, and he drove into her in one long exquisite thrust.

She cried out, her back arching on the desk like a bow, her hair rioting around her head, her eyes stuttering closed.

Hate was definitely underrated, he thought, as he braced her hips and drew slowly back, feeling involuntary muscles protest around him, try to keep him, seeing her eyes flicker open, confused and bereft and wanting more.

He gave her more. The second lunge took him deeper. She cried out again and this time when she bowed her back, he scooped her up from the desk so that she was sitting astride him, her breasts pressed against his chest, her legs curled around him and as he lifted her hips and let her fall, it was his turn to groan.

She needed no help to find the rhythm. She damn near set about setting it. She might have looked stunned before, but now she squirmed her bottom in his hands and braced herself on his shoulders, levering herself higher, letting herself take him in, increasing the speed, driving it, while her mouth worked at his throat, sharp teeth finding his flesh, every nip and bite timed to perfection, agony melding with ecstasy.

She was like a wildcat in his arms, untamed and unleashed, and it was all he could do to hang onto her while she used her body against him—all he could do to hang on, full stop.

Until she pumped him one too many times and any vestige of control vanished as he exploded inside her, the fireworks of her own orgasm ricocheting, magnified, through his.

Gasping and sweat-slicked, he hung on, her limbs heavy now, her head low on his chest, carrying her through an adjoining door to his suite. Awkwardly he pulled back the covers and then eased her onto the bed, where she closed her eyes and sighed into the mattress.

No tears, he thought, no recriminations? Half expecting both. That was a bonus. Though there probably wasn't a whole lot more to say after *I hate you.*

Unless it was *I still hate you.* He smiled as he headed for the bathroom, already contemplating round two. He could think of worse ways to spend the night. That first coupling had been so fast and furious, already he was contemplating the pleasures to be had in other, slower, methods. Next time he would take his time. Explore her body in more delicious detail. Next time he would be the one to set the pace.

He caught a glimpse of his neck and shoulder in the mirror, shocked at first at the marks of her teeth standing out bright and red. He smiled as he fingered them, the skin tender where she had left her brand. He remembered her biting him, but nowhere near this many times. Foremost in his mind had been the ecstasy. She was a tigress all right. Wild and untamed, and as unexpected as her surprise arrival tonight.

But then not entirely a surprise. Clearly he'd hit on the one thing that she held dear.

She'd surprised him with her vehemence. She'd been so prepared to walk away from her mother—to let her face the consequences of her overspending and be thrown out onto the streets if it came to that. He'd misjudged the relationship between mother and daughter badly. But then he'd only really had Lily's side of it to go by and in Lily's world, it was all about Lily.

But suggesting Lily ask her first husband to help, that had been a stroke of genius. Finally he'd found the one person Valentina did care about—the one she would do anything to rescue—even if it meant sacrificing herself to his bed.

Everyone had their price, it was said. He had just found Valentina's.

He padded back from the bathroom to find her curled kitten-like into a ball in the centre of his bed, her breathing even and deep and fast, fast asleep.

So much for round two.

Bemused, he climbed in alongside. She stirred and murmured something in her sleep and he wasn't planning on holding her but she curled herself against him and settled back into her dreams on a sigh.

It wasn't what he'd been expecting. He wasn't used to holding anyone when he slept. He wasn't used to anyone sleeping on him. Certainly not a woman he wasn't done with yet. He willed away an erection that was more wishful thinking than opportunity and tried to relax. She was warm and languid and, for all her muscled leanness, she was soft too, and in all the right places.

Relax? Fat chance.

But at least he could think about what might happen when she woke up.

One month she'd agreed to stay.

It had seemed more than ample when she'd suggested it. He'd only ever planned to keep her long enough that she thought she was safe, that maybe he might provide the answer to all her needs. Long enough to feel secure and so comfortable in her position as Venice's first lady that she wouldn't see it coming. Her public humiliation.

And then he remembered what had happened in his study and how she had turned the tables on him and milked him for all he was worth. And the thought of thirty nights of Valentina hating him and proving it every night in his bed—or on his desk for that matter—seemed nowhere near long enough.

She came to gently, slowly, with the strange feeling she was still moving, and for some vague period of half-sleep, she believed herself back on the plane.

Until logic interceded and she realised that last-minute bargain economy seats on passenger planes did not come complete with sublime mattresses and pillows big enough to land that plane on.

Venice.

She sat up in bed, realising she was hearing the chug of a passing vaporetto rather than the constant hum of jet engines, and she remembered the argument with her mother, and an explosive session on Luca's desk. And then—*nothing.*

She dropped her head into her hands.

What had she done?

She lifted the covers. Of course she would be naked. And of course it had been no dream. She'd performed some kind of amateur striptease in front of him. She'd offered herself as a conscientious objector instead of him taking her as an unwilling sacrifice. And she remembered a desk and the feel of him inside her.

How could she ever forget the feel of him inside her, the sense of fullness and completion and the exquisite side effects of friction?

In three years she hadn't forgotten and nothing, it seemed, had changed. Her memories were true.

But she couldn't for the life of her remember a bed. Luca's bed, she recognised, not only by his lingering scent and the presence of a jet-black hair on the pillow, but the sheer masculinity of the room, as if he'd stamped his personality on it by the sheer force of it. She'd slept in his bed and he'd slept alongside her and, surprisingly, that act seemed even more intimate than the one they'd shared on the desk.

But where was he now?

A robe lay on the coverlet. Silky and jade-coloured. She snatched it up and wrapped it around her in case he suddenly appeared. Strange, to feel shy after what she'd done last night, but she wasn't practised in negotiating a deal while taking off her clothes. She'd never expected to seal one in such a way. But last night fury had given her courage to do what she had done; rage had given her purpose. This morning she was still angry with both her mother and with Luca, but now there was wonderment too at her brazen behaviour. Not to mention a little fear, for what she might have let herself in for.

One month of sleeping with Luca Barbarigo. Thirty nights of sex with a man who knew how to blow every fuse in her body and then some. Thirty whole nights after three years of abstinence—she shivered—it was almost too much to think about. It was almost, so very almost, *delicious.*

The silken robe whispered against her breasts. Her nipples tightened into buds. She could not let him see her like this. He'd think she was primed and ready for a second course. He might even be right to think that.

But Luca didn't arrive and the only sounds she heard were the sounds of Venice coming from outside the windows. The only movement she felt seemed to come from the very foundations, the gentle sway of time and tide.

And only then did she notice the clock on a mantelpiece. *Three o'clock?*

She'd slept the entire day?

She padded from the bed and located the bathroom, and then found the study through another door with no sign of her pack and no trace of anything that had happened last night, the floor cleared of abandoned clothing, the desk restacked with pens and phones and files and so neat that she wondered for a moment if she'd dreamed it all. But no, there was no dreaming the tenderness of muscles rarely used. No dreaming the sense of utter disbelief—wonderment—at what had occurred.

For her hastily concocted plan—a plan made in fury and rage—a plan that in the cold light of day seemed impossible and unimaginable—had come off.

She'd come to Luca Barbarigo not as his victim, but as his seducer. Laying before him her own terms, not being forced blindly to accept his. And she seemed to recall it working. Or so she'd thought before sleep had claimed her. Some seductress she'd turned out to be.

She was still searching when there was a knock on the door, and Luca's manservant swept in a few seconds later, bearing a steaming tray laden with both coffee and tea, together with an assortment of rolls and pastries. If he was unfamiliar with finding women in his master's bedroom, it didn't show.

She clutched the sides of her robe more tightly around her. She needn't have bothered. His eyes avoided landing anywhere near her. She shoved aside the niggling thought that this wasn't the first time, but there was no point dwelling on it. Her deal was for one month. She didn't care who filled his bed all the other nights of the year.

'Would the *signorina* like anything else?' he asked, putting down the tray and moving towards the window. 'Signore Barbarigo said you would be hungry.'

It's so long since I've eaten, she wanted to add. 'That looks perfect,' she said, because the contents of the tray looked more than adequate, but also because clearly somewhere along the line she'd been promoted to something a little higher than something that the cat had dragged in.

'Where is the *signore*—Luca, I mean?' as the man swept rich vermillion curtain after rich vermillion curtain open, splashing light into the room with every broad sweep of his hands.

'Signore Barbarigo is of course, at his offices at the Banca d'Barbarigo.'

'Of course,' she said, but the sound came out wrong. She hadn't meant to sound disappointed. She'd meant to sound relieved. Hadn't she? It wasn't as if she expected him to hang around and wait until she woke up. After all, he'd got what he wanted, hadn't he? And he knew she wasn't going anywhere for at least a month. He knew where to find her when he wanted her.

The thought rankled, even though she'd known what she was letting herself in for.

'If there is nothing else?'

The valet was standing at the door, ready to take his leave. 'Actually there is.' She felt herself colour when she remembered where she'd left them. 'I can't seem to find my clothes.'

'The clothes you were wearing last night?'

And left scattered indecorously across the study floor? He didn't have to finish the sentence so she chose to answer it with another question. 'And my bag. I couldn't find it.'

He showed her into an adjoining dressing room and pushed against a panel in a stuccoed wall that she'd assumed was just a wall, revealing a closet secreted behind. And there, tucked away, was her pack, with yesterday's clothes folded neatly on a shelf. 'Your clothes have been laundered and pressed. Unfortunately the brassiere could not be saved.'

'Never mind,' she said too brightly, secretly mortified as she remembered the snap and tear when Luca had all but wrenched it from her, while Luca's valet seemed not to blink an eyelid at the carnage.

'The rest of your wardrobe should be here shortly.'

She frowned, searching for meaning. 'But I left nothing at my mother's.'

'The *signore* has organised a delivery for you. I am expecting it at any time.'

A delivery? To replace one plain old bra that had seen better days? He needn't have bothered, she thought, rummaging in her pack after the valet had departed. It wasn't as if she travelled without a spare.

Half an hour later she emerged from the bathroom wearing a floral miniskirt that she loved for the way it flirted around her legs and a cool knitted top and found the delivery man had been. Or men, plural, because it must have taken an entire team to cart the lot filling the dressing room wardrobe.

A veritable boutique was waiting for her, dresses of all descriptions, from day dresses to cocktail dresses to ball gowns. She flicked through the rack, many of the items still in transparent protective sleeves, along with racks of shoes—one pair for every outfit, by the look of it—and the drawers filled with lingerie of every imaginable colour.

And not a T-shirt bra in sight.

So much for imagining Luca wanted to replace her bra. He wanted to replace her entire wardrobe. She almost laughed. Almost. Because it was ridiculous.

Not to mention unnecessary.

More than that. It was downright insulting.

She pulled open the bedroom door and called for the valet. Who the hell did Luca Barbarigo think he was?

She was writing an email to her father on her clunky old laptop, pounding at the space bar that only worked when it wanted to, when the double doors to the living room opened. She didn't have to turn her head to know it was Luca. The way her heart jumped and her skin prickled was enough to tell her that. And the way heated memories of last night and a certain desk jumped to centre stage in her mind, she was grateful to have something to focus on so she didn't have to look at him until she'd wiped all trace of those pictures from her eyes. She banged her thumb once again on the space bar, trying to appear unmoved, while feeling the weight of his gaze on her back.

'What are you wearing?'

'I'm trying to get this space bar to work. It sticks all the time.' She pounded on the key again, hoping it covered the thump of her heart and this time it worked and she managed to rattle off another few words before she noticed her fingers were on the wrong keys and she'd written nonsense.

'No. Not, what are you doing. What are you *wearing*?'

The correction took her by surprise. She forgot the email and looked down at her simple outfit and then around at him. She almost wished she hadn't. The dark business suit and snowy white shirt made him look powerful. The five o'clock shadow darkening his olive skin turned that power into danger. Or was that just the way his eyes narrowed as they assessed her? She might just as well be a butterfly pinned in a display cabinet, being examined for the colour of its wings. Being found wanting.

'Just a skirt and top.' And she half wondered whether he was still seeing her in those jeans, as she edged them down over her hips. Had he been expecting to find her wearing them again? Had he been hoping for a repeat performance? She shivered in anticipation—suddenly half hoping… 'Why do you ask?'

'What happened to the clothes I ordered? Did they not arrive?'

Oh. She'd forgotten the clothes. She swivelled out of her chair and stood, keeping hold of the desk behind her, solid and strong. Sitting down he loomed too tall and imposing, but standing up wasn't as easy as it looked. Not when it looked as if the Furies were about to descend upon her. 'They came.'

'Then why aren't you wearing something from that collection?'

She hitched up her chin. 'How do you know I'm not?'

He snorted. 'Believe me, Valentina, it shows.'

'So what's wrong with what I'm wearing, anyway?'

'Nothing, if you want to look like a backpacker. Go and get changed.'

'Excuse me? Since when did you tell me what to wear?'

'Ever since you agreed to this deal.'

'I never—'

'You made your conditions known last night, if I recall rightly. I remember nothing about choosing what you wear being one of them. In which case…'

'You can't make me—'

'Can't I? I have a dinner reservation in one hour. At one of the most exclusive restaurants in Venice. Do you expect to accompany me wearing those rags?'

'How dare you?' They weren't rags to her. Maybe nothing in her wardrobe cost more than fifty dollars, maybe they weren't weighed down in designer labels, but they were hardly rags. She bundled up her outrage and fired it straight back. 'Anyway, those clothes you had delivered…'

'What about them?'

She allowed herself a smile. 'I sent them back.'

'You *what*?'

'You heard me. I sent them back. I didn't ask for them, I didn't want them, so I told Aldo to send them back.'

Luca stormed to the door. 'Aldo!' he yelled, his booming voice echoing around the palazzo, before turning around and striding across the room, eating up the length of it in long powerful strides, wheeling around when he reached the end. 'I can't believe you would do such a stupid thing.'

'And I can't believe you would order clothes for me like I was some kind of doll you want to dress up and play with!'

He stopped right in front of her. 'You will be seen on my arm. You will look the part.'

'As your strumpet, you mean. As your whore!'

'I didn't see you complaining last night when you

agreed to this deal. You seemed quite willing to spread your legs for me then.'

The crack of her palm against his cheek filled the room, the resultant sting on her hand a mere shadow of what he must be feeling.

He rubbed his face, his cheek blooming dark beneath his hand. 'You seem to have an unfortunate habit of slapping me, Valentina.'

'What a coincidence. You seem to have an unfortunate habit of provoking me.'

'By calling a spade a spade? Or by buying you clothes and insisting you wear them? Most women would not object. Most women would be delighted.'

'I'm not most women and I am not your whore. And I agreed to share your bed, yes. But that doesn't mean I'm happy to be paraded on your arm like some kind of possession.'

'Did you expect to stay one month chained to my bed? While I must admit the idea appeals on some primitive level, given I have your agreement to this arrangement, it seems such drastic measures will not be necessary.'

'What a shame,' she snapped. 'I imagine someone like you would get a real kick out of that.'

'I don't know,' he countered. 'Why would I restrict you to my bed when you have already shown such willingness for spontaneity?'

Aldo coughed at the door, signalling his presence, and two heads swivelled simultaneously. Tina wanted to curl up and die while Luca might just as well have been talking about the weather for all the embarrassment he showed. *'Prego,'* said Luca. 'I'm looking for the clothes that were sent, Aldo. The ones Valentina says she had sent back.'

'They are downstairs in the studio. I thought, under the circumstances, it might be wise to wait.'

Tina forgot her embarrassment. 'What? I told you to send them back. You told me you'd take care of it.'

He bowed his head. '*Scusi.* If that is all?'

'No,' Tina said, 'that's not all—'

'What Aldo is saying—' Luca interrupted '—is that I am master of this house. You are a guest and an honoured one, but you would do well to understand that I make the decisions here. Not you.'

He turned to his valet. '*Grazie*, Aldo. Perhaps you might be so good as to select a few outfits for our guest to choose from. It seems designer fashion is not one of her strong points. She may need your assistance.'

'I don't want to go out.'

'Find her something sexy, Aldo,' he said, as if she hadn't spoken. 'Cocktail length would be perfect. High heels. Choose something that shows off her figure. I want every man in that restaurant to be salivating for her and every woman to be hating them for it.'

Aldo bowed and turned, a man on a mission, clearly unsurprised by his master's bizarre request and equally clearly expecting her to follow meekly along now that they had both been given their orders.

She stood her ground. 'And meanwhile,' she said, 'while all these people are busy either drooling or planning to murder their partners, what will you be doing?'

His smile returned, and a flare of something hot and dangerous in his dark eyes sent a bolt of heated anticipation coursing straight through her. 'I'll be imagining bringing you back here and tearing whatever it is you're wearing right off you until you are lying naked and spreadeagle on my bed.'

She shivered at his words, even as his smile widened dangerously. 'And now,' he said, his white teeth almost glinting, 'so will you.'

CHAPTER SEVEN

How was a girl supposed to think of anything after that?

Numbly Tina followed Aldo down the marble staircase, wishing she had a way to prove Luca wrong and wipe that knowing smile from his face, but there was no denying the delicious thrill of anticipation that had accompanied Luca's dark promise. And it was a promise, for it could hardly be called a threat. Not when her blood fizzed at the knowledge that in a few short hours he wanted her back in his bed.

Was it wrong to look forward to sex with a man that you hated, who held you hostage to a debt you hadn't yourself incurred? But maybe that was the wrong question to ask, for that question led to more questions, and all kinds of answers she didn't want to think too much about.

Maybe it was simply better to ask if it was wrong to look forward to an act that you knew would blow your mind and your world apart—an act that your body hungered for on a scale you had never known—an act you had already agreed to undertake for one entire month and so what was the point of asking anyway?

Surely that was the better question.

It felt better, from where she was standing.

'This one,' said Aldo, intruding into her thoughts as he handed her a dress, feverishly intent on his task and already searching for the right accessories as she took the hanger. He soon found what he was looking for and before she knew it she was back in her dressing room and wearing a dress that fitted as if it had been made for her.

And in spite of her protests that she didn't want any of Luca's clothes and her order to send everything back, she adored the dress the moment she slipped it over her head. It felt delicious and sinful and decadent all in one go.

Cocktail length, the cobalt satin dress skimmed her shape without a ridge or seam in evidence beneath—perhaps because she was wearing gossamer-thin silk underwear instead of her usual plain, cotton bras—or perhaps because it was so superbly right for her, the dress nipping in at the waist to make the most of her curves, hugging her shape like a caress.

Aldo had somehow even managed to conjure up earrings to match, sapphires set with diamonds that sparkled when they caught the light, the blue stones echoing the rich colour of her dress. A touch of make-up and a simple uptwist of her hair were all she needed to do herself, and even she was astounded by the results. The rich colour of the dress did something to her eyes, turning amber into gold, although maybe it was the thoughts of what would happen later that seemed to turn them molten.

'You look amazing,' Luca said when she emerged, his rich deep voice working its way down to her bones, and he made her believe it. When she looked into his dark eyes, she felt his desire. When he took her hand to step down into the water taxi, she felt the spark of his need ignite her own.

Mad, she thought, as he finally let her hand go so she could precede him into the interior; she must be mad to feel this schoolgirl breathlessness, this overwhelming sense of anticipation. It was not as if she was going on a date with a man she wanted to be with. It was not as if they hadn't already made love. In fact he was really nothing to her but an obligation—thirty days and nights to spend in his bed—a deal made with the devil.

But knowing that was somehow still not enough to stop the racing of her pulse as he ducked his head and curled his long body onto the leather divan alongside her. Knowing that was no protection against the lure of his signature scent or the sheer magnetism of his body heat. In fact, logic seemed pathetically irrelevant when the devil looked like Luca Barbarigo.

The water taxi cruised slowly down the Grand Canal, past yet more examples of Venice's architectural treasures, and out past the crowded St Mark's Square with its magnificent Doge's Palace and towering Campanile. Across the basin, the church of San Giorgio Maggiore and its bell-tower stood majestically on their own island.

She'd come here not as a tourist. She'd come to Venice with no thought of sightseeing, but it was impossible not to drink in the sights and be awed by the spectacle.

How could anyone remain unmoved, when the shifting view revealed such a feast for the eyes with every turn? And then Luca turned his head and she caught his profile and the feasting continued.

Such sculpted perfection, she thought, such classical chiselled features. He belonged here in Venice, amongst the beautiful and the magnificent. He was a part of it. And as she drank his dark beauty in, she wondered…

Would their son have grown up to look like him?

Pain, sharp and swift, lanced her heart and so suddenly that she gasped with the intensity of it. A single tear squeezed from each eye and she had to cover her mouth with her hand to prevent her grief escaping via that route.

'What's wrong?' he asked, but all she could do was shake her head as she remembered.

Their tiny son.

Born too early to save. Born too late not to love. A child lost.

A child his father knew nothing about.

'It's nothing,' she lied, knowing that the only good thing she had taken from their baby's premature death was the relief that she would never have to tell him—that it didn't matter because she would never see him again.

But where was that relief now that she was here in Venice, forced to share a month with the father of that child? Where was the certainty now, that what she had decided back then was right?

She'd been a fool to ever believe it would be that easy. For the relief had turned to guilt, certainty had turned to fear, as the secret she had tried to lock away now hung over her like the sword of Damocles.

How could she begin to tell him the truth about their child now? Where would she start?

'It's the wake from the vaporetto,' he said alongside her, misinterpreting her distress. 'We're over it now.'

She nodded and smiled thinly, and wondered if she ever would be.

The water taxi berthed a few minutes later down a side canal at a plushly canopied hotel landing.

'Feeling better?' he asked, as he handed her out of the taxi.

'Yes.' And she was, if only because she was surprised by his concern. It wasn't one of the things she associated with the man. Arrogance was a given. Lust she expected. But concern hadn't figured on her list of Luca's character traits. Then again, maybe he was just worried that his playmate might be too ill to play games tonight. And that sounded so fitting that she even managed to dredge up a smile. 'Much better, thank you.'

Through an elegant arched doorway and the hotel lobby opened up like an Aladdin's Cave. Ceilings soared, magnificently decorated with gold leaf, while pink marble columns stretched high to reach them and a wide red carpeted staircase wound around the walls on its way heavenwards.

'It's stunning,' she said.

'You are.' And when she turned to look at him, he simply gestured around. 'Every head is turned your way. Hadn't you noticed?'

No. 'If they are, it's because I'm with you.'

'They're all wondering who you are, it's true,' he told her as he led her towards the magnificent staircase, 'but every woman in this hotel wishes she looked like you.'

'It's the dress,' she countered, needing to change the subject, before she started believing him. 'However did you know what size to have delivered?'

'Wouldn't you expect a man like me to know what size his lover wears?'

She shivered. His lover? That seemed too personal. Too intimate. Theirs was a business arrangement. A deal. So she schooled her features, aiming for cool and unaffected and definitely uncaring. 'Clearly you've had plenty of practice to be so good at it.'

'Clearly.' His smile widened. 'Does that bother you?'

'Why should it? I don't care who you sleep with. I don't want to know.'

'Of course,' he said. 'Although perhaps I am not so expert as you would like to believe. Aldo found your clothes. The tags were still readable apparently. But only just.'

Another reminder of her wanton behaviour. Yet another reminder of the age of her clothes. And she had no comeback either, other than to blush. So she concentrated on the stairs beneath her feet and just hoped her face didn't clash with her dress.

The restaurant ran the length of the building, half enclosed, half terrace, all understated elegance with red upholstery and cream linen tablecloths, with touches of gilt for highlights around artfully placed mirrors. Heads turned as they passed, men greeted Luca like an old friend, women preened for him and stared openly and questioningly at her. He swept through the room like a rolling wave, refusing to be distracted for longer than a second, even when it was clear that he was being welcomed to share someone's table for the evening.

Clearly Luca had other plans.

Through wide glass doors they were led onto the broad terrace, where Luca's table stood waiting for them at the far corner, boasting uninterrupted views over the San Marco Basin and the Gulf of Venice. Below them tourists paraded along the Riva degli Shiavoni enjoying the balmy September evening while water craft darted across the basin lit up like fireflies.

Luca sat back in his seat and smiled. The views from the terrace were sublime, it was true, but then his view was even better. He hadn't lied. She looked amazing tonight. There was something about the colour of her cat-like eyes. And there was something about the colour of that dress, the way the shadows danced across it in the light whenever she moved. His fingers envied those shifting shadows and itched to dance their own way across her skin. 'Are you hungry?' he asked as they were handed their menus. He was, but what he wanted to feast upon had nothing to do with his stomach.

She'd left him hungering for more last night. He'd imagined a second course before leaving for work, but she'd been so deeply asleep this morning that letting her sleep had seemed the far wiser action. He wanted her wide awake when he made love to her again. And this time he wanted her to last all night.

This night.

The thought was as delicious as anything offered on the menu, which suddenly seemed too long and filled with far too many courses. He lost interest in the choices, returned to watch her instead, enjoying the tilt of her head and the curl of slim fingers angled around her menu.

'A little,' she said, her eyes drifting upwards, widening when they caught him watching her. She swallowed and he watched the slight kick of her chin and the movement down her throat. 'Is there something special you can recommend?'

Plenty. But if she was talking food—he skipped straight to the main courses, already impatient to be home. Surprised a little by how much. 'The monkfish is excellent here, or there is always the rabbit.'

Something flared in her eyes, something challenging, as if she could read his thoughts. 'I think the beef,' she said, and he smiled.

'Excellent choice,' he said, thinking she would need it and ordered for them both.

Sparkling prosecco arrived, poured into glasses spun with gold. 'A toast,' he said, lifting his glass to her. 'To…' She arched one eyebrow, waiting. He smiled, a long, purposeful smile. '…anticipation.'

Her expression gave nothing away. Only her eyes betrayed the fact she felt it too, this thread between them, as fine as that trace of gold spun in their glasses, pulling inexorably tighter. 'To anticipation,' she echoed, a husky quality infusing her voice as she lightly touched her flute to his.

Giddy.

She hadn't even had one sip of the wine and she already felt giddy. But how could she not? The setting was sublime, the view magical and the man opposite was looking at her as if she was more tasty than anything on the menu.

And no matter what she thought of him, she could not help but like the way he looked at her and what it did to her body. She liked this delicious heat simmering under her skin and the way his eyes warmed her from the inside out. She liked the way he seemed impatient to have this meal over with when he had been the one who had insisted on coming out. There was something empowering about his need, something that meant he didn't hold all the cards.

Yes, she had agreed to his deal. She was his for the month, it was true, but did he not realise that by dressing her up and turning her into something worthy of his attention he was handing her a decent measure of his power?

All she had to do was play her part. It wasn't hard. Whatever she thought of Luca Barbarigo and his ruthless determination to get his own way, there was no hardship in anticipating the pleasures of the night to come. Just as there was no hardship in anticipating the pleasures of walking away one short month from now.

Oh yes, she'd drink to anticipation.

'So this is where we make small talk,' Luca said, breaking into her thoughts. 'Where we sit and converse like two civilised people when there is somewhere we would both rather be and something we would both much prefer to be doing.'

There was no need to ask what he would rather be doing, not when his dark eyes were thick with desire. But if he wanted small talk… 'Maybe we could talk about the weather,' she suggested. 'It's a beautiful night.'

'The weather does not interest me.'

'No? Then we could talk about the view. You could point out the places of interest. There seems to be no shortage of those.'

He shook his head. 'I could do that. But that would be dull. We would just be marking time. I would rather talk about you. How long is it since that night? Two years? More?'

That night. What an appropriate way to put it. 'Three years come January.'

'So many.' He took a sip of his wine and sat back, his dark eyes searching hers. 'Which begs the question: what have you been doing all that time?'

Well, now there was a simple question. How to find a simple answer for all she had been doing?

Nursing a bruised ego.

Discovering that she was pregnant.

Grieving the loss of that child.

Hating...

She picked up her water glass, a tumbler that bore the swirling logo of the restaurant, clearly made locally in Murano, and she wondered that, for all her vast collection, her mother had never managed to find anything near as simple or as beautiful. She studied the piece so that she didn't have to look at the man sitting opposite. She stared at it so he wouldn't know how much his questions unsettled her. 'Working on my father's property, mostly.' The mostly was important. She wasn't about to confess that for the first few months she'd been holed up in a friend's one-bedroom flat in Sydney while her life lurched from one turmoil to the next.

'What kind of property? Lily said something about wool?'

She buried the spike of resentment that rose at the mention of Lily and the farm in the same sentence. 'Yes. Sheep and some cropping. Lucerne mainly.' She looked around at their watery world, lined with buildings that went back at least five centuries. Some years the farm didn't see rain, the dams dried up and the sheep turned red with dust. The last drought had lasted so long, some local kids had grown up thinking sheep were supposed to be red. 'It's different from here,' she said, making a massive understatement, 'that's for sure.'

'So you're close to him, then. Your father.'

She shrugged. 'Of course. He was the one who brought me up after Lily walked out.' Whereas Lily, she thought, had been a some time holiday destination—her visit usually coinciding with a wedding. There'd been two more of those before her marriage to Eduardo. One to a Swiss ski school owner. Another to an Argentinian polo player. Neither of them had lasted either.

Funny, she thought, how life ran in circles sometimes.

She'd met Luca at her mother's wedding to Eduardo. By then, aged seventeen, she'd well and truly realised that her mother's life was as empty and pointless as they came. And by then she was hardly going to fall into bed with someone who happened to be Eduardo's nephew, even if he was the most perfect male specimen she had ever laid eyes upon and even if he made no bones about his attraction to her…

Luca snapped a breadstick, jolting her back to the present. 'I have trouble picturing Lily on a farm.'

'They should never have married. I'm sure she imagined she was going to end up some rich farmer's wife and play tennis and drink tea all day.'

'But it didn't turn out that way?'

She shook her head. 'She hated it, apparently—the flies, the heat—she left when I was six months old. Just packed up and left Mitch with a baby and a hole where his heart had been.'

'It seems—' he hesitated a moment, as if searching for the words '—an *unlikely* match. Someone like Lily with someone who works on the land.'

'I think their differences were what attracted them to each other. She was the original English flower, on holidays to visit an old maiden aunt. He was the rugged Australian right down to his leather workman boots and as exotic to her as she was to him. When they met at some charity event in Sydney, it was lust at first sight.' She sighed. 'In normal circumstances it would have run its course and they would have both gone back to their separate worlds but Lily ended up pregnant with me and before you know it they were married. Pointlessly as it turned out.'

'You don't approve?'

'I don't think an unplanned pregnancy is any reason for a marriage! Do you?'

Maybe she'd sounded too strident. Maybe her question had sounded too much like a demand because she needed him to agree with her. But across the table from her, Luca merely shrugged instead of agreeing. 'I am Italian. Family is important to us. Who's to say if it's the right or wrong thing to do?'

'Me,' she said, knowing that if he knew—*if he had only known*—he would think differently. 'I've lived my life knowing their marriage was futile, a disaster from start to finish. I would never do that to a child of mine. I might be Lily's daughter, but I am not Lily!'

'And yet here you are, still picking up after her.'

'I'm not doing this for Lily,' she hissed, with rods of steel underpinning her words, 'but you threatened to bring my father into this and there is no way on this earth I am going to let you suck him into Lily's nightmare. He's worked hard for every cent he has and I won't let him lose any of it on her account!'

She was breathless after her outburst. Breathless and breathing fire, but she was glad too, that he had reminded her of all the reasons she hated him, that he thought he could manufacture the result he wanted by manipulating people and using them for his own ends.

'Do you realise,' Luca asked, leaning forward and cradling his wine glass in his hands, 'how your eyes glow when you are angry? Did you know they burned like flames in a fire?'

She sucked in air, blindsided by the change in topic, but more so because she had expected anger back in return. She had been prepared for Luca to fight, expecting him to fight, if only to defend his low actions. Whereas his calm deliberations and an analysis of her eye colour had knocked the wind from her sails.

'I was angry,' she said, uncomfortable and unnerved that he could find things about her that nobody else had ever told her. Things that she herself didn't know. 'I still am.'

'It's not just when you're angry though,' he continued as their meals arrived, the waiter placing their plates with a flourish before disappearing on a bow. 'They glowed like that last night when you came. I look forward to seeing them burn that way for me again tonight.'

She wasn't sure which way was up after that. The meal passed in a blur, she ate and the beef melted in her mouth, but five minutes after her plate was whisked efficiently away, she couldn't have described how it tasted. Five minutes after he said something, she couldn't have remembered his words. Not when her whole being seemed focused not on the meal, but on the senses he stirred and by the knowledge of what would come afterwards.

Every word he spoke stroked her senses. Every heated look stoked the fire burning deep inside her belly. Every single smile had the ability to worm its way under her skin.

God, but he looked so good when he smiled. Generous lips swept open to reveal white teeth. Not perfect teeth, she noted with some satisfaction, for one eye tooth angled and hugged too close to one of his front teeth to be absolutely perfect. And yet somehow that made him more real than make believe. Somehow that only worked to make him more perfect. And still he looked so good that logic got spun on its head and she might even imagine for one infinitesimal moment that…

But no.

She brought herself up with a thump. Took a drink of *frizzante* water to cool her heated senses. There could be no imagining. Not where Luca Barbarigo was concerned.

But there could be tonight.

An entire month of tonights.

Her body hummed as dessert was short-circuited for coffee.

Anticipation built to fever pitch in her veins, as lingering to enjoy the view was short-circuited for the promise of pleasure.

The boats were still darting across the basin like fireflies; most of the tables around them were still full, when Luca had clearly had enough. 'It's time,' he said throatily, and there seemed nothing left to say when the hunger in his eyes told her all she needed to hear.

He guided her through the restaurant, the touch of his hand at her lower back no more than the graze of his fingertips, and yet every part of her body seemed focused on that spot, as if he'd tied a ribbon between them that kept her close.

And this time Luca all but ignored the greetings that were called out to him. He ignored the eye contact that would ensure recognition and guarantee acknowledgement. He stopped not once in his quest to get her out of the restaurant and down the stairs and into the waiting water taxi.

For me, she told herself. He is avoiding them for me, and that knowledge was as empowering as it was intoxicating.

All the more empowering given he had forgiven a debt—a massive debt—for the pleasure of her company.

And a question that had been niggling away at her wanted answering.

What was this all about?

Why her? Sure, her mother owed him a fortune, but surely there were plenty of women who would be prepared to grace Luca's arm and his bed for however long it took without sacrificing a cent of her mother's debt. Why did he want her? What was his game?

On the taxi he suggested they stand outside and watch the moving light show along the canal, and he took her hand and led her through to the rear deck. 'You're frowning,' he noticed, wrapping his arms around her as she held onto the rail as the taxi moved away from the dock.

She stiffened a little. 'Maybe because I don't understand you.'

She felt him shrug against her back. 'What's so hard to understand?'

'Why you want me.'

'I'm a man who likes women,' he said, peeling her away to spin her around to face him. 'And you are—' his eyes lowered, raking over her, and they might just as well have been raking hot coals over her skin '—unmistakably all woman. Why wouldn't I want you?' He leant down closer, his lips drawing closer, and fear the size of a football kicked off in her gut. She turned her head away.

'Don't do that. Don't kiss me.' People who liked each other kissed. People who were in love.

'Why not?'

Because kisses were dangerous. You could lose yourself in a kiss, and she didn't want to be lost with Luca Barbarigo.

'Because I hate you and I don't think you particularly like me that much. It just seems false.'

'And sex doesn't?'

'Not when it's just sex.'

'Just sex. Is that what you thought we were having last night—just sex?'

'What would you call it?'

'Mind-blowing. Earth-shattering. Maybe even some of the best I've ever had.'

She gasped, her eyes searching his face for laughter, finding no trace. It had been like that for her…but for him? And whether it was the sudden acceleration of the taxi as it joined the main canal, or because she didn't want to prevent it, but this time when his mouth came closer—so close that his lips brushed hers—all the air disappeared from her lungs in a rush of heat, leaving a vacuum that could be filled only by him.

He filled that vacuum with the more solid press of his lips upon hers. He filled it with the taste of him in her mouth.

Coffee and wine and heat combined in a knee-trembling cocktail that threatened to bring her undone, and only his arms around her kept her standing. And as his lips made magic against her mouth, it occurred to her that she'd been right to worry, because a girl could not only get lost, but drown in a kiss like that.

She was already drowning—in sensation. There was nothing between them but silk and cloth and the knowledge that when they came together it would be explosive.

His hands moved over her like both a caress and a demand. His kiss promised her his soul while it wrenched free her own.

She could not afford to let go of her soul.

She turned her head away and pushed against his chest, determined to show him she was unmoved while she still could, before she got lost for ever in his kiss. Before she believed its promise.

He let her go and she spun away, grabbing hold of the railing like a lifeline. 'I wish you hadn't done that,' she hissed.

'Do you?'

'Yes! Because this whole thing still makes no sense, when you could have your pick of any woman in Venice. Any woman anywhere for that matter and without having to blackmail them into the deal.'

'But I didn't want any other woman,' he said, peeling her away from the railing and back in his arms. 'I wanted you and you alone.'

'Lucky me.'

He laughed. 'And would you have come to me if I hadn't blackmailed you into my bed?'

'No,' she said breathlessly, still trying to grapple with the sense of it all. 'I wouldn't have come to you if you were the last man left on earth.'

'Then there you have it,' he said with another of those deadly smiles, his lips pressing to her forehead. 'You gave me no choice. Your not wanting it makes having you all the more satisfying.'

CHAPTER EIGHT

ANGER was good. Anger she could harness and mould and shape into something to sling right back at him. And it would not be simpering submission, but forged in hatred, and it would be slung back at him on her terms.

Anger coloured desire and turned it into a weapon. Anger shaped passion and turned it into something much more dangerous, much more lethal.

So that by the time the water taxi arrived back at the palazzo she didn't feel fearful or afraid or vulnerable.

Instead she felt stronger than she had ever done. She had survived his kiss, she had suffered his taunts, and if he thought he was going to take and take freely of her, he was very much mistaken.

Because she'd make damn sure she would take more than she would give. No, there was nothing to fear from Luca Barbarigo.

Aldo greeted them discreetly at the water door, just as discreetly evaporating as Luca ushered her upstairs, every slight caress of the hand at her back a siren's call to her senses while ratcheting up her simmering resentment; every silken whisper of his presence both a caress and a curse.

And it didn't matter any more that she didn't understand

whatever game Luca was playing. Because she knew what was expected of her as they climbed the stairs.

And what was expected of her was the easy bit.

It was just sex, after all, whatever he wanted her to believe. It wasn't as if she needed to put on a special performance. All she had to do was take off her clothes and get into bed with him. Nothing to it.

Dinner had been interminable. He'd wanted to be seen. He'd planned to give time for his dinner companion to have been photographed and image searched and found to be someone with links to him. But still it had taken too long—far too long when what he most wanted was to have her in his bed. But it had been necessary.

It shouldn't take anyone curious too long to work out.

His uncle's widowed wife's daughter.

She wouldn't be hard to trace, not with today's search technology. Soon there would be articles in newspapers and magazines. Soon the world would know she was living in his palazzo and that they were an item.

A few more outings and the papers would blow it out of all proportion and wedding bells would be predicted and gambled upon.

And she would start believing it herself.

That was when she would be the most vulnerable.

That was when she would be starting to believe the fairy tale. And she would. Even now, for all her protests of hating him, she melted in his arms like wax.

She was his.

She'd made that plain last night with her impromptu striptease, when she'd offered herself to him on his desk. She'd made that plain the way she'd stunned herself with the force of her orgasm.

Soon she would forget all about hating him and start believing in dreams.

And that was when he would unceremoniously dump her.

But that was later.

First there were more carnal pleasures to be enjoyed.

Starting now.

The bedroom lighting was low, the air body temperature, the wide bed turned down on both sides. He smiled as he closed the door to the suite behind him, watching the seductive sway of her hips as she headed across the room, liking the way the dress clung to her curves. He liked her in that dress. It would be such a shame to tear it off.

Then again…

'Where are you going?'

She stopped, looked over her shoulder at him. 'My dressing room. I'm guessing you expect me naked for tonight's performance.'

'What? No impromptu striptease tonight?' he asked, flicking open the top button of his shirt, tugging at his tie. 'No office antics?'

She blinked, golden eyes glinting and hard, watching him remove the cufflinks from his shirtsleeves. She made a move to walk away.

'Come here.'

'I don't take orders from you.'

'Come here,' he repeated, his voice velvet over steel.

'Why? So you can rip this dress off like you would… like the caveman you like to keep dressed up under those fancy Italian suits of yours? Nobody's fooled, Luca, least of all me.'

'Maybe you should come here and find out.'

Fire flared in her eyes, shooting flames straight to his groin.

'I like this dress, I don't want it ruined.'

'I like it too, as it happens. Maybe I just want the pleasure of peeling it from your body.'

'Fine,' she snapped, 'have it your way.' But there was a husky edge to her grudging agreement that signalled she wasn't as in control as she made out, even as she crossed the room and spun around in front of him, presenting her back.

Not so fast, he thought. Instead of reaching for the zip, he put his hands on her shoulders and dipped his mouth to the place where her throat met her shoulder. Her gasp was his reward, her tremor was his vindication.

'You see,' he murmured against her throat, 'even the caveman can play nice.' And she trembled again.

He ran his hands down her arms, taking his time to drink in the feel of her smooth, toned limbs, curling his fingers possessively around hers before starting the long road up. There was plenty to enjoy. There was plenty of time. Last night's lovemaking had been so rushed, he'd missed a lot.

And there was so much more to explore. His fingers found the catch of her zip and he slid it slowly down, letting just one fingertip trail a line down the skin beneath. Another involuntary gasp from his reluctant playmate and the temptation to slide his hands underneath the fabric and ease it over her shoulders and be done with it was almost too much.

Almost.

Instead he spun her around and cradled her jaw in his hands, lifting her face towards his. Her lips were parted, her breathing shallow and fast and her amber eyes swirled with confusion. There was resentment there and heated anger, but there was a flicker of vulnerability too in those amber depths, a flicker that was almost endearing.

'Where is your caveman now, Valentina?' he asked, searching her face, watching her mouth and those lips, parted and panting and just begging to be kissed. He wasn't about to disappoint them. He dipped his head and brushed her lips with his and sighed with the simple, exquisite pleasure.

Just sex, she told herself. It was just sex. His kisses meant nothing, the tenderness meant nothing.

It was just sex.

It meant nothing.

So why did it feel so very good?

His lips moved over hers like a piece of music, a symphony that built and grew and slowed to tender lows and soared to great heights and everywhere in between.

His hands traced a path down her throat. She felt the brush of silken straps over her shoulders and the slip of her dress as it fell to the floor. She felt air that cooled and caressed her naked breasts and turned her nipples even harder.

She felt his hands slide down her bare back and pull her against him.

She felt him, long and hard against her belly. Felt the aching need for him between her thighs and her hand moved of its own volition, unable to resist the temptation to curl her fingers over that rigid column.

Breath hissed through his teeth. He lifted her from the circle of her dress and into his arms, took three long strides and tossed her into the centre of the waiting bed. Chest heaving as if he'd run a marathon, he looked down at her on the bed, eyes raking down over a body clad in nothing but gossamer-thin shreds of silken underwear, a pair of killer heels and a pair of earrings, while his hands were busy pulling off his shirt, his shoes, his trousers.

She could not take her eyes from him, from the lean and

sculpted perfection of his body, from the heart-stopping size of his erection as it sprang free. Looking at him made her blood fizz and her flesh ache.

And then he kneeled alongside her on the bed and slipped off first one shoe and then the other, kissing the soles of her feet, sliding his hands up her legs to catch the scrap of silk that was her underwear, sliding it down and tossing it over his shoulder.

'Did anyone ever tell you,' he said, his voice thick with need as he gazed down upon her naked form, 'that you look amazing in sapphires?'

She was sure she would have remembered if someone had, but right now there was no space for raking up memories, no room for anything that might have happened in the past. This moment was all about what was happening now.

He lowered his head and put his mouth to her breast, drawing it in, rolling his tongue around her nipple while one hand swept down her body from neck to breast to thigh to knee, his long fingers spread wide, missing nothing, leaving no part of her untouched, leaving no part of her to his imagination. Through his scorching touch, he drank her in until she felt more liquid than solid, her senses flowing, eddying.

She shuddered under the heated assault, her senses alive, her need building like a whirlpool; spinning as he rained hot kisses down her belly; spinning as he spread her legs wide and dipped his head between her aching thighs.

The first touch of his tongue was electric, sending her arching against the mattress. She cried out, something incomprehensible—meaningless—other than as a reflection of the exquisite agony of his hot tongue circling her pulsing core, and his clever lips toying with that screamingly tight bud of nerve endings. And all the while the whirlpool built inside her, sucking her deeper, rendering her senseless, her world ever shrinking, until it consisted of nothing more than a spinning sea of sensation.

She was lost in that sea. Cast adrift. And still it wasn't enough. Still she needed more.

'Tell me that you want me,' he murmured, sensing her distress, and she felt his words on her secret flesh.

Her head thrashed on the pillow. 'I hate you.'

He caught her between his lips, suckled harder.

'Tell me that you want me.'

'I want you,' she half cried, half sobbed, the confession wrenched bodily from her as he continued to work magic with his mouth, as the circling storm inside her wound tighter and inexorably tighter like a coiled spring until she would die with it.

'I want you now!'

And his mouth was gone and she had one moment of relief, one moment of loss, before she felt him nudge at her core and drive himself home.

It was the trigger she needed, the trigger that released that achingly tight coiling spring and sent her soaring. She exploded around him as he held her and filled her and completed her.

'You should hate me more often,' he joked as she came down from the high, her body slick and hot and humming in secret places.

'I do,' she said, panting, hating him right now for his ability to do that to her, to turn her incendiary with his clever hands and clever mouth.

'Good,' he said, moving inside her, making her gasp as she realised he was still hard. 'Keep on hating me.'

She could do that. But there was no time to tell him, no time to get her breath back. He leaned back, lifted a lifeless leg and flipped her neatly onto her front before she knew what was happening, all the time still buried deep inside her.

Shock rendered her speechless, not only at his sudden manoeuvre, but at the tightening and dance of muscles she'd thought wasted, muscles that welcomed another chance to play.

Large hands anchored her hips as he drew back and she hated his leaving almost as much as she hated him.

Maybe more.

He took his own sweet time coming back, inch by excruciating inch until she thought she would go mad with want, until he was seated deep inside her, his thighs pressed hard against hers.

She sighed with the exquisite fullness of it. Oh God, he felt so good this way, so deep.

And when he moved it was even better. He started slowly, inviting her into the rhythm of his dance, taking her with him. His hands grew hungrier, sliding down her spine, curling around a breast, slipping around a thigh to stroke her sensitive nub. He was everywhere around her. He was inside her. He possessed her.

The rhythm built, the pace increased, the slide of flesh against flesh set to the sound of the slap of skin against skin and the feverish need for air as he wound her need around him, tighter and tighter than it had been before and left her teetering on the edge of a precipice.

He paused, leaving her on the brink. She heard a sound like a whimper, needy and desperate, before she realised it had come from her own throat.

And then it was his turn to cry out—a cry of triumph borne of pain—as he thrust one last desperate time and sent her to that place where hate and want coalesced in a fireball that consumed her.

He followed her over the edge, pumping his release and catching her to ride the wave together.

I hate you, she thought, as he collapsed alongside and gathered her close.

I hate you, she thought, as a single tear rolled down her cheek. *I need to be able to hate you.*

But after what they had just shared, the sentiment rang hollow and empty.

CHAPTER NINE

LUCA couldn't remember the last time he'd slept late. Not that he hadn't woken earlier. But this morning she'd stirred too and she'd been warm and malleable in his arms and it had been inevitable that they'd made love again.

But then instead of rising like he'd planned, he'd fallen back to sleep. If Aldo hadn't woken him with a subtle knock at the door, he'd still be sleeping.

'What time is it?' he asked as Aldo placed a tray of coffee and rolls on a table. Beside him Valentina stirred, still sprawled on her stomach, her hair in disarray around her head, testament to the riotous night they'd spent rediscovering each other's bodies. How many times had they made love? Was it four? Or five? He'd lost count along with his sleep.

'Ten o'clock,' the valet said in response to a question Luca had forgotten he'd asked. 'I wouldn't have disturbed you but Signore Cressini called and said he needed to talk to you.'

'Matteo called?' he asked, lashing a gown around himself while Aldo opened the curtains.

Aldo nodded. 'He said it was important.'

He left the room as Valentina lifted her head from the pillow and sniffed. 'Mmm, coffee,' she muttered before dropping her head back on the pillow and Luca smiled and reached for the pot, filling them both a cup while he wondered what Matteo wanted.

Mind you, he owed his cousin a call—he had, after all, put paid to the spending habits of his best customer. Matteo, no doubt, wanted an update.

He reached for his phone and immediately thought better of it. He was already late for the office and it wasn't as if there was anything pressing or that there weren't any number of bright young things who wouldn't be happy to cover for him for the day. Besides, right now bright autumn sunshine was flooding the room with light. Late September and the weather was still holding. Any time now the storm clouds of a European winter would come sweeping down from the north, and the heavens would turn grey and dark and open up and turn Venice from a watery wonderland into a rain-lashed water world.

Maybe he should to take a little time out while his guest was here before that happened. A run out to the island of Murano wouldn't take that long. It would make for more photo opportunities of them together for a start. And then afterwards there'd be time for a late lunch and a long afternoon siesta. He might not be Spanish, but there were plenty of reasons to like the practice. Making love in the middle of the day was one of them. Thirty nights could stretch a little that way.

But not if she was going to spend it all sleeping. He pulled off the covers and slapped her bare rump, almost tempted to linger at the sight of her creamy flesh. 'Wake up, Sleeping Beauty. I've got plans for you.'

She didn't exactly jump at his suggestion of visiting Murano and his cousin's glass factory. The glass that formed her mother's addiction was not something that held her fascination—she'd seen enough of it at Lily's palazzo to last a lifetime. And it wasn't as if she needed a reminder of how her mother had been manoeuvred into debt—yes, because she was feeding a compulsion of her own making—but also by probably two of the best in the business.

After all, who else to feed a glass-infatuated woman's habit but a financier who wanted to steal her house out from under her and his cousin, the man who owned the factory and who supplied her fix?

What worried her more, she reflected as she tied back her hair and swiped gloss over her lips, was spending time with Luca—time when they were not making love. It was one thing to share his bed and his nights—that had been the deal she'd made. She just wasn't sure she wanted to share his days. Because she needed time alone. Time to think. Time to regroup.

Time to put into perspective their love-making, to bundle it up in a box marked *meaningless* and shove it under the bed until the next night.

It was harder to do than she'd thought. Harder to separate the passionate Luca from the hated. Harder to hold herself together, even when she was coming apart.

No, she didn't need to be reminded in the daylight hours of the tender caress as he'd stroked her skin or the way he'd turned her molten with one flick of his clever tongue. She needed the lid put on that box and put on firmly and for it to be all tied up tight.

But he'd insisted. Why? To rub her nose deeper in her mother's mess by taking her to the scene of the crime? Surely he knew better now than to think that she cared enough about Lily's foolishness for that.

So he'd insisted and she'd relented. Besides, the weather was sunny, the skies clear blue, and she'd found a gorgeous floral print sundress that was just begging to be worn. Why shouldn't she see something of Venice while she was here?

And if Luca could put up with her daylight company for a few hours, she could hardly confess that she was afraid to do the same. She would just have to work harder to keep a lid on that box.

And when all was said and done, what was she afraid of, anyway? Actually liking the man? There was no chance of that, not after all the things he'd done.

Luca was in his study making calls when she emerged, so she pulled out her laptop and curled into a chair to try to finish the email to her father. He would be wondering what was happening over here and when she was planning on coming home. She was wondering how best to tell him without having him launch himself halfway around the world brandishing a shotgun to save his daughter from the clutches of the evil Luca.

She smiled at the thought as she pounded on the space bar, trying to imagine him in Venice, surrounded by water, practically living on top of the water. He'd taken her to the beach for a holiday once, when she was ten. A wide, sandy beach framed by rocky cliffs and wild waves and an endless, endless sea. He hadn't stopped staring at the sea for days, and when she asked what he was looking for, he'd just shaken his head and muttered, 'All that water.'

A bubble of sadness rose up unbidden to sully the memory and she felt a familiar pang of loss. And then the space bar stuck again and she wrote a line of jibberish and she cursed, distracted. The damn key was getting worse. No question about it.

'You look good enough to eat.'

Her mouth went dry. She swallowed, suddenly reminded of another time, another feast, the lid well and truly ripped from the box.

Was he thinking about last night too?

She took her time closing her laptop, wishing away the burning in her cheeks. She didn't dare meet his eyes. 'I didn't hear you come in.'

'I'm not surprised. Is that a computer or a brick you're banging away on?'

'It's all right,' she said, putting it down, happy to talk about anything other than the reason for her blushing. 'It does the job. Most of the time. It's just seen better days, that's all.'

He came closer, picked it up and tested its weight with one hand before discovering he needed two. 'It's seen better centuries.'

'It's fine,' she said, even though it weighed a ton and was so slow it was good for little more than the occasional email.

He grunted and put it down. 'The driver's here, if you're ready.'

Beyond the crowded canals of Venice, the driver opened up the engines. The sleek timber craft's nose leapt clear of the water, the boat skipping over the surface of the lagoon in a rush of power.

Luca asked her if she wanted to go inside, but it was exhilarating standing at the back of the vessel, the wind tugging at her hair, and she shook her head. Besides, the view outside was just too good. There was something about seeing Venice from the water, buildings standing where by rights there should be none, rising vertically from the lagoon like a mirage.

But the city was real. Just as the man standing at her side was real. Heart-stoppingly, devastatingly real, when she thought about their love-making last night; ruthlessly, unscrupulously real when she remembered why she was here, and if there was a mirage anywhere, it was this game they were playing, pretending to be lovers.

He'd told her last night he wanted her so badly that he would use her mother's debts to blackmail her into his bed. Then, with the wick of anticipation already lit and burning down towards their inevitable coupling, it had almost seemed reasonable. Today logic demanded a better explanation. Because she wasn't that special. What was really going on?

He put a lazy arm around her shoulders and she looked up at him. 'Why am I here?' she asked, her words tugged away by the wind. 'The real reason this time.'

His eyes were masked by dark glasses. 'Don't you want to see Murano?'

'No,' she said, not knowing if he had deliberately chosen to misunderstand her question, 'I don't mean that.' But, before she could clarify, he squeezed her shoulders and pointed ahead. 'Look, we're almost there.'

They slowed and landed at a small dock where a man stood waiting for them. He waved as they pulled alongside and she had no doubt who he was. Cousins could be brothers, both lean and long-limbed and good-looking enough for a dozen men. 'Matteo,' called Luca as he bounded onto the dock. The pair embraced before he turned to offer Tina his hand.

'And this,' he said as she joined him on the deck, 'is Valentina Henderson, Lily's daughter.'

Matteo smiled and greeted her like a traditional Italian, a kiss to each cheek before standing back, a wide smile on his handsome face. 'Lily's daughter, yes, I see it, but much more beautiful too. Do you share your mother's passion for our local glass, Valentina?'

'No,' she said, ignoring the compliment and hoping to knock on the head any hope he might hold that he had gained himself a new client. 'It holds no interest for me at all.'

'Valentina has—' Luca looked at her and smiled '—other passions, don't you, Valentina?'

One day she would grow out of blushing, she swore, as she tried to look anywhere but at the two men standing opposite. Maybe just not today.

'Come,' said Matteo, clearly enjoying the joke as he clapped his cousin on the shoulder, 'let's see if we can change that.'

She wasn't about to have her mind changed. Not when she was led into the large warehouse room, warm from the heat of at least four fiery kilns. Men worked there, doing whatever it was they did, but it was the chandeliers she noticed hanging from the warehouse ceiling, magnificently ornate and totally incongruous examples of the glassmakers' craft in the yawning airspace above her, that made up her mind.

So this was where her mother had found her inspiration for her disparate collection.

'If you would excuse me,' Luca said, 'I have to talk with my cousin. Would you mind waiting here for a few minutes? The glassmakers are about to put on a show. You might enjoy it.'

She raised her eyebrows. They did a show? Bring it on, she thought cynically, but still she welcomed this brief respite from Luca's presence. She welcomed the chance to breathe in air not tainted by the scent of him in space he didn't own. So she let herself be led to a small stand of tiered seating where a couple of other family groups were already seated, ready and waiting. There was space in the front row still, and she sat down and almost immediately wished she hadn't.

A toddler was sitting on the floor to her side, his mother

nursing an infant behind him, his father on the other side. The child looked up at Tina as she sat down, all huge eyed, mouth gaping, clearly wondering who she was to be invading their space.

He would be about the right age, she reasoned with a sizzle of recognition, feeling her stomach churn. *Their son would have been about the same age as this child.*

She looked away, thought about leaving, her palms suddenly damp with sweat before his big dark eyes drew her back like a magnet.

Dark eyes. Long lashes.

She had seen her baby's eyes open, and they had been dark too, like this child's. Like his father's.

The boy looked up at his mother, who was still busy tending the baby, before he looked back at her, blinking.

She smiled thinly, trying to will away the churning feeling in her gut, trying not to hurt herself more by thinking about their son growing up. But it was impossible.

She'd read the books, even before he was born. He would be two now. Full of life. Inquisitive. Driven to explore his new world. Sometimes challenging.

This child was no doubt all of those things and more. He was beautiful as he looked at her, his expression filled with question marks, and so distracted that the toy bear in his hands slipped from his grasp to the floor.

Without thinking, she reached down and scooped it up and for a moment, when he realised, he was all at war, mouth open with brimming outrage, little arms pumping fisted hands.

Until she handed back the toy and he looked almost shocked, before his face lit up with a smile as he clutched the teddy to his chest and squeezed it for all it was worth.

And that smile almost broke her heart.

Somehow she managed a tentative smile back, before

she had to wrench her eyes away from the child who reminded her of too much, from the child who was not hers.

From the ache in her womb that would never let her forget.

Tears pricked her eyes as she looked plaintively up at the high ceiling, to where the gaudily coloured chandeliers hung bold and totally shameless, mocking her, and she wished to hell she'd never come.

A collective gasp from the crowd and she turned to see one of the workmen wielding a rod tipped with molten glass dancing at its end. White-hot and fringed with red it glowed, fresh from the fire, stretching down long in its melted state before the artisan used a blunt implement and smacked it short.

The blob seemingly complied, buckling under the commands of a stronger force, melting back into itself.

From then on it was a dance of heat and fire and air, the sand turned molten glass, the rod spun and spun again over rails of steel, cooling the liquid magma until it was cool enough to be tweaked, a tweezer here and there to tug upon the glass and pull a piece outwards, a prod there to push it in, seemingly random.

She watched, but only half-heartedly, determined not to be impressed, finding a welcome distraction when she noticed the craftsman was wearing nothing on his feet. Molten glass and bare feet, she thought with horror, but happy to think of anything that would provide a distraction from the child alongside her, watching now from his father's knees in open-mouthed fascination.

She clasped her hands together tightly on her empty knees.

And then, as she watched, the bare-footed artisan's purpose became clear. A leg, she realised. Two legs, fine and slender. A roundness and then two more legs, with a twist to make a neck before the tweaking continued, the artist's movements now almost frenetic, working the glass before it cooled too much and set before he was finished.

She gasped when she realised. A prancing horse had emerged from the glass, with flowing mane and tail, and mouth open to the air, alive.

With a snap it was free, set down on a table where it stood balanced on its back legs and tail, front hooves proudly held high in the air.

She applauded louder than anyone and, when the glass had cooled, the artisan presented it to her.

'For the beautiful *signorina*,' he said with a bow, and she held the creation still warm in her hands, blinking away tears she hadn't realised she'd shed.

'It's magical,' she said, turning it in her hands, marvelling at the detail—the tiny eyes, the shaped hooves—the glass glinting in the light. 'You are a true artist.'

He bowed and moved away, back to the kiln for his next work of art.

She turned to the family alongside, who were all watching with admiration and held it out to the mother. 'You take it, please,' she said to the startled woman, pressing it into her hand. 'For your son, as a memento of this day.' *For the tiny child who could never receive her gift.*

The woman smiled and thanked her, the husband beamed and the little boy just blinked up at her with those beautiful dark eyes.

She couldn't stay. She fled. She strode away, feigning interest in a cabinet filled with numbered jars of coloured sand, with curled samples of glass hanging from a board, her back to the family, arms wound tight around her belly, trying to quell the pain. Trying not to cry.

'Did you enjoy the demonstration?' she heard Matteo ask. 'Did you like your souvenir?'

She had to take a deep breath before she could turn and face anyone, let alone them. She plastered a smile on her face that she hoped looked halfway to convincing.

'She gave it to the boy,' called the artist before she could say anything, gesturing with a grin towards the family, who were all still gathered around admiring it.

Luca laughed and slapped his cousin on the back. 'I told you she doesn't like glass.'

His cousin shrugged as a woman came running from another room, a large bunch of flowers in her arms that Matteo took from her, thanking her for remembering.

'Thank you for delivering these,' he said, handing Luca the flowers. 'Tell her I will come and see her soon.'

They left then, Matteo kissing her cheeks again as he bade them farewell, before the boat set off, the flowers lying inside on one of the long loungers.

'Who are they for?' she asked, curious, when Luca hadn't spoken for a while.

He looked straight ahead, his jaw grimly set. 'Matteo's mother. It's her birthday today but he has to take his daughter to the hospital for an appointment. He won't have time to visit her.'

'Where does she live?'

'There,' he said, pointing to a walled island she belatedly realised they were heading towards.

She shuddered. 'But surely that's…'

'Yes,' he said grimly. 'Isola di San Michele. The Isle of the Dead.'

CHAPTER TEN

THE brick walls loomed larger the closer they got, dark walls with white detail in which was set a Gothic gateway framing three iron gates.

Behind the walls the heavy green stands of cypress and pine did nothing to dispel the sense of gloom and foreboding.

She shivered.

'You must have been here before,' he said as the boat pulled alongside the landing.

She shook her head. 'No. Never.'

He frowned. 'I remember now. You didn't come to Eduardo's funeral.'

She sensed the note of accusation in his voice. 'I didn't make it in time. My flight had engine trouble and was turned back to Sydney. By the time I arrived, the funeral had already been held and Lily was barely holding herself together. There was no chance to pay my respects.'

He studied her, as if trying to assess if she was speaking the truth. Then he nodded. 'So you can pay your respects now, if you wish. Or you can stay with the boat if you prefer. Some people are not fond of cemeteries.'

'No,' she said, thinking nothing could be more forbidding than those imposing gates. Nothing could be worse than waiting to the accompaniment of the endless slap of water against the boat. 'I want to come, if you don't mind. I liked Eduardo. I'd like to pay my respects.'

Once again he paused, as if testing her words against what he knew of her. Then he gave a careless shrug. 'Your choice.'

Inside the imposing walls she was surprised to find the gloom fall away, replaced by a serenity that came with being in a well-tended garden. The sounds of motors and the chug of passing vaporettos seemed not to permeate the thick walls. Only birdsong and the crunch of gravel underfoot punctuated the silence. Here and there people tended graves, or just sat under the shade of the cypress trees in quiet reflection.

Luca led the way, past rows of neat graves adorned with marble cherubs and angels and freshly cut flowers. Everywhere she looked seemed to be bursting with the colour of fresh flowers.

He carried the bunch in his arms almost reverently. Flowers might soften a man, she thought, but not Luca. They only served to accentuate his overwhelming masculinity. Big hands, she thought, and yet so tender, the way they cradled the flowers.

Like he might cradle a child.

What would have happened had their child lived? If he had not been born too prematurely to be saved? Luca would not have welcomed the news that their one night of passion had ended with more than a face slap and that he was a father, but would he have wanted to meet his child? Would he have cradled him in those big hands as gently as he cradled those flowers and smiled down at him? Could he have loved him?

She dragged in air, shaking her head to escape the thoughts. There was no point in thinking what-ifs. Nothing to be gained but pain layered on pain.

Through different garden rooms they walked, and around them the closely packed lines of graves went on.

'It's quite beautiful,' she said softly, so as not to interrupt the pervasive sense of calm. 'So peaceful and well maintained. More like a garden than a cemetery.'

'Their families look after the graves,' he said, turning down a side path. 'They are all recently deceased. Space is limited, they can only stay here a few years before they are moved on.'

She remembered reading something of the sort. Probably around the time Eduardo had died. It seemed strange in one way, to disturb the dead and move their remains, but then again, who wouldn't want a chance to rest, at least a while, in such a beautiful setting, with the view of Venice just over the sea through the large iron gates?

'Matteo's mother died recently then?'

'Yes, two years ago, although space is not an issue for my family,' he continued, leading her towards a collection of small neoclassical buildings. 'The Barbarigo family has had a crypt here since Napoleonic times when the cemetery was created.'

Of marble the colour of pristine white sheep's wool, the crypt stood amongst others, but apart, more the size of a tiny chapel, she felt, no doubt demonstrating the power and wealth of his family through the centuries. Two praying angels, serene and unblinking, overlooked the gated entry, as if watching over those in their care, guarding who went in and who came out. Tiny pencil pines grew either side of the door, softening the look of the solid stone.

She took the flowers for him while he found the key and turned the lock. The door creaked open and cool air rushed out to meet them. He lit a candle either side of the door that flickered and spun golden light into the dark interior and took the flowers from her. And then he bowed his head for a moment before stepping inside.

She waited outside while he said some words in Italian, low and fast, she heard Matteo's name and she knew he was talking to his mother, passing on his cousin's message.

So true to his word.

So honourable.

So...*unexpected.*

She didn't want to hear any more. She breathed in deep and moved away, faintly disturbed that it should bother her.

It was peaceful and quiet in the gardens, dappled sunlight filtering through the trees, leaves whispering on the light breeze—so serene and unpopulated when compared to the crowded Centro, and she thought what an amazing place Venice was, to have so many unexpected facets, so many hidden treasures in such a tiny area.

She found another treasure amongst the trees—a gravestone she'd happened upon with a sculpture of a child climbing a stairway to heaven, fresh flowers tied onto his hand, an offering to the angel smiling down on him, waiting patiently for him at the top. She knelt down and touched the cool stone, feeling tears welling in her eyes for yet another lost child.

'Would you like to pay your respects now?'

She blinked and turned, wiping a stray tear from her cheek, avoiding the questions in his eyes. 'Of course.'

She followed him into the tiny room, the walls filled with plaques and prayers to those buried here over the years.

'So many,' she said, struck by the number of name plates. Flowers adorned a stone on one side—Matteo's mother, she reasoned.

'Eduardo is here,' he said, pointing to a stone on the other wall. 'His first wife, Agnetha, alongside.'

She moved closer in the tiny space, Luca using up so much of it, and wishing she had stopped to buy a posy of flowers to leave in the holder attached to the stone.

'I'll leave you to it,' he said, and moved to go past her. She stepped closer to the wall to let him, and it was then she noticed the names on the wall alongside. 'Your grandparents?' she asked and he stopped.

'My parents,' he said, stony-faced, pointing to a spot lower down on the wall. 'My grandparents are in the row below.'

He turned and left her standing there watching his retreating back. His parents? She looked again at the plaques, saw the dates and realised they'd died on the same day as each other nearly thirty years before.

Luca must have been no more than a few years old…

He was cold and distant when she emerged a few minutes later, his sunglasses firmly on, hiding his eyes. 'Ready to go?' he said, already shutting the door behind her, key to the lock.

'Luca,' she said, putting a hand to his arm, feeling his corded strength beneath the fine fabric of his shirt. 'I'm sorry, I had no idea that you'd lost both your parents.'

'It's not your fault,' he snapped.

'But you must have been so young. I feel your grief.'

He pulled his arm away. 'You feel my *what*? What do you know of my grief?'

The pain of loss sliced through her, sharp and deep as he walked away. 'I know loss. I know how it feels to lose someone you love.'

More than you will ever know.

'Good for you,' he said, and headed back towards the boat.

* * *

She found a box waiting for her on their return, on the table next to the bed. 'What's this?' she asked. 'I didn't order anything.'

'Open it up and find out,' he snapped, before disappearing into the bathroom, the first words he'd spoken since the cemetery. His silence hadn't bothered her during the journey home. Instead she'd welcomed it. It restored him to the role of villain. It balanced any glimpse of tenderness he might have shown—the reverent way he'd carried the flowers for his aunt—the quiet respect he'd shown when he'd entered the crypt.

It helped her forget how good he could make her feel in those moments where she could put aside thoughts that this was all a pretence, all a hoax.

And she didn't need to find things to like about him. She liked him being cold and hard and unapproachable and totally unforgivable.

It was better that way, she reasoned, as she tackled the box, looking for a way in.

Easier.

Necessary.

She found the end of one tape, ripping it from the seam of the box. Found another and swiped it off, opening a flap and then another layer of packing.

No!

Luca returned, his tie removed, his shirt half unbuttoned, exposing a glimpse of perfect chest. She tried not to look and failed miserably as he kicked off his shoes. And then she remembered the box.

'Where did this come from?'

He shrugged, and pulled his shirt off over his shoulders. 'You needed a new computer.'

'My computer is fine!'

'Your computer is a dinosaur.'

'You're a dinosaur!'

He paused, halfway to tugging off his trousers, and in spite of herself, she couldn't help but feel a primitive surge of lust sweep through her as she considered all the reasons he might be undressing, her mind lingering longingly on one particular reason... 'And there was me thinking you considered me a caveman.'

'Dinosaur. Caveman,' she said, trying not to notice the bulge in his underwear, trying to hide the faltering sound of her voice, 'It's all the same to me. All prehistoric.'

'Surely not the same,' he said with a careless shrug of his shoulders that showed off the skin over the toned muscle of his chest to perfection as he turned towards her. 'I would have thought a dinosaur would be lumbering and slow, and awkward of movement. Whereas a caveman could have more fun, don't you think, clubbing women over the head to drag them back to his cave to have his wicked way with them.'

She swallowed as he reached out a hand and stroked back the hair from her brow, winding a tendril of it around his finger. It was hard to think with a naked man standing in front of her, his proud erection almost reaching out to touch her. The caveman taunting her with his club. Making her hungry for him. 'You're right,' she said. 'You do the caveman thing particularly well.'

He smiled, and tugged on the curl of hair he had wound around his finger and drew her mouth closer to his. 'Surely not the only reason you're here, Valentina? Don't you enjoy being with me?'

'No,' she said, as he tugged on her hair and drew her still closer to his mouth. She held her breath. 'I'm counting down the days until I will be free.'

He smiled as if he didn't believe a word of it. 'In which

case,' he said, 'I'd better make the most of the days that are left.'

He pulled her face to his, his lips meshing with hers, insistent but still coaxing, inviting. And when he finally took his mouth away and she breathed in again it was to have her whole body infused with his scent and his taste.

He sighed. 'I'm sensing a problem here.'

It was impossible to make sense of his statement through the thick fog of desire clouding her brain. She licked her lips, tasting him on her tongue. 'What problem?'

He put a hand to her breast, cupped the aching weight of her through her dress. 'You're wearing far too many clothes.'

And she almost sighed with relief as she gave herself up into his kiss. Of all the problems in her life right now, an excess of clothes was one problem she could fix.

She'd imagined he wanted quick sex, fast and hot and furious. What he did was make love to her as if she were as fragile as that tiny glass horse.

His hands were slow and hot, his mouth scorchingly tender, his tongue an instrument of exquisite torture, and with all these things he spun a web of silken arousal around her, so that when she came, it wasn't wrenched from her or like being caught in the maelstrom of a storm, but almost like an admission. A confession. A giving up of herself to him.

She lay there panting, eyes open and afraid, staring at the ceiling.

Because sex was one thing. She could handle sex. Rationalise it. Treat it as a currency if she must. And she could stick it in that imaginary box under the bed in the cold light of day and shove the lid on and divorce herself from what was happening.

But giving herself up to him, losing herself in him when

she knew she was going to walk away empty-handed in a few short weeks, that scared her.

It wasn't just the sex that was making her feel this way, she knew. It was Luca himself who was changing. Showing concern when she felt shell-shocked on the boat—buying her a new computer because her old one was decrepit and inefficient. She knew he could afford it a million times over—she knew a few hundred euro would mean nothing to him—but it was the fact he'd even bothered that cut her deepest. For he didn't have to do those things. He didn't even need to find Lily an apartment when she already owed him so much.

Why did he have to appear half human when she wanted him to stay one hundred per cent monster? Why did he make it so hard to keep hating him?

She wanted to hate him.

She had to hate him.

She closed her eyes and sent up a silent entreaty to the gods. Because if she was ever to walk away from here with her head held high and her ego intact, she needed a reason to hate him.

Now, more than ever.

He should take more days off. He lay in bed listening to the rumble of his stomach—he would have to get up and have lunch soon, he supposed, before it turned on him and ate him alive—but there was something so utterly decadent about spending the middle of the day in bed. Especially when you had a good reason not to get out of it.

Like Valentina.

Idly he stroked her hair, listening to her soft breathing as she lay alongside him. He liked that she didn't feel the need to chat incessantly or ask him if it was good for him. What he liked even better was watching her eyes when she tipped over the edge. He shifted one leg, making room. God, but just thinking about it made him hard all over again.

He should do this more often.

Then again he could, at least for the next month. Or what was left of it. Plenty of time yet. Maybe even tomorrow. Thinking of which…

'I'm seeing your mother for lunch tomorrow,' he told her. 'Would you like to come with me?'

He felt her body tense. Wary. 'Why are you seeing my mother?'

'There are some papers to be signed, to finalise the transfer of the properties, the palazzo to me, the apartment to your mother.'

'And you want me there why exactly?' She sat up clutching the sheets to her chest, her golden eyes bright with argument and accusation. 'So you can gloat about how clever you are in front of us both?'

He blinked. Where had that come from? He'd thought her half asleep and she'd come out fighting.

'I thought you might like to see your mother.'

'Like hell, you did.' She clambered from the bed, dragging the bedding with her, uncaring that she was pulling the sheets from him at the same time. He grabbed hold and pulled back and the sheets snapped tight between them, caught in the crossfire, stopping her in her tracks.

She spun around, trapped in the tangle of sheets. 'You've got what you wanted. You've tricked my mother out of her house and why—' she waved her hand around the room '—when you obviously need another house like a hole in the head? You've got a playmate in your bed for a month because it's what *you* wanted and bugger what anyone else wants. What kind of sick person are you that you need to see us together like some kind of weird trophies?'

'I thought you'd like to see your mother,' he said through a jaw so stiff it could have been made with the same Istrian stone that formed the foundations of Venice itself. 'I know I'd give the world to be able to visit mine somewhere other than in a cemetery.'

She seemed to cave in before his eyes, the fight evaporating from her in a heartbeat. 'Luca,' she said softly, making a tiny move closer to the bed.

'Forget it,' he said, throwing off the sheet. 'It was a lousy idea anyway.'

He stormed off to the bathroom. *So much for enjoying a lazy day in bed.*

She didn't see Luca after that and she suspected he'd taken himself back to the office. She couldn't blame him. She'd jumped down his throat at the suggestion of visiting her mother as if it was for his spurious pleasure to have them in one room at the same time. But then, after such tender love-making, after his impromptu gift, the foundations under her seemed to be shifting and she'd needed to see him as the villain. She needed to reclaim the anger she'd felt when she'd marched into his study and practically demanded he make love to her.

Instead she almost felt sorry for the way she'd snapped at him.

She felt as if she'd let him down.

She felt as if she'd let herself down and failed some kind of test.

Crazy.

It wasn't as if she even cared what he thought of her. Her relationship with her mother was her business. He wouldn't know about the way they'd last parted, the argument that had sent her foaming mad to his door to almost dare him to take her. He wouldn't know the fractured history that lay festering like the worst of Venice's rotting piles between them.

But his gut-wrenching admission that he'd adore the opportunity to see his mother if only she were alive…

And regardless of what she thought of Luca, regardless of her justification for acting this way, it shamed her that her relationship with her own mother was so appalling.

Maybe there was just cause given the events of the last few days. But equally maybe, now that the dust had settled on the deal that had been made, perhaps while she was in Venice she should try to heal that rift, even just a little.

She heard her father's words come back to her, the rationale he'd used when she'd tried to wiggle out of coming to Venice in the first place.

'She's still your mum, love...you can't walk away from that.'

She's still your mum.

Maybe her dad was right. Maybe Luca was right. Maybe she should make an effort after all.

While she was still in Venice.

While she was lucky enough to still have a mother.

CHAPTER ELEVEN

'YOU'RE sleeping with him, then?'

Carmela had her back to Lily as she poured Tina a cup of coffee and threw her a sympathetic smile. Tina smiled back, appreciating the shared moment, regretting just a little that it had to be with the housekeeper rather than her mother, but then again, so far the visit had been surprisingly pleasant, given all the places it could have gone. They'd talked about the weather, and all about the new apartment Lily had visited just this morning. The biggest surprise had been finding the boxes and tissue paper scattered around the floor and learning that Lily was already sorting through her trinkets and thinking about which pieces to keep and which to sell through consignment with a local gallery owner. Tina's unexpected visit and coffee had come, she'd said, as a welcome respite.

So yes, it was progress of sorts, that Lily was accepting the inevitability of her move, even if there was remarkably little so far in the 'sell' box.

Of course, she was still railing on about the injustice of the whole thing and how could she possibly fit into a 'tiny' six-room apartment? But Tina was still glad she'd come, although she'd always figured she was never going to dodge the bullets for ever.

'It's true, Lily,' she admitted, wondering how many

other daughters were interrogated so openly on who they might be having sex with. But then, what was the point of avoiding the truth? It wasn't as if it was a secret. Everybody in Venice who wanted to know must know. 'I'm sleeping with Luca.'

Her mother sniffed as she sat back in her chair, and it was hard to tell whether she was pleased or disappointed. It was obvious she wasn't surprised. 'So, will it lead anywhere this time, do you think?'

That one was easier to answer. 'No.'

'You seem very sure.'

'I am sure.'

'What about Luca?'

'He's sure too. We're both sure. Can we just leave it at that?'

'Of course,' she said, putting her cup down on its saucer with barely a clink, and Tina hoped that was the full stop on that particular conversation.

But then her mother sighed. 'And yet,' she continued, 'it seems to me that for a man to come back for a second bite of the cherry, there must be something he finds… compelling about a woman. I mean, if a man comes looking for an encore, then surely he must be—'

'—looking for an easy lay. Leave it, Lily. I don't want to hear it. It's not leading anywhere. At the end of the month I walk away. Luca stays here.' She shrugged. 'End of story.'

'Well, it just seems such a waste. I don't know why you're not taking advantage of this arrangement. You could do a lot worse for a husband.'

Tina rubbed her forehead. Why did headaches so often coincide with visits to Lily? 'I'm not actually in the market for a husband.'

'But if something were to happen…'

'Like what? Like a baby, you mean? I'm hardly going

to fall pregnant. Not twice to the same man. I'm not that stupid.'

Her mother shrugged and stood, looking around the room. 'It's lovely you dropped by, but I should do some more sorting, I suppose. Luca is sending an army of men to do the chandeliers, but I don't want them touching my precious ornaments and there's such a lot to do.' She looked up at her daughter, a decided gleam in her eyes. 'I don't suppose you could help?'

Tina blinked, not really surprised that her mother would ask for help, more surprised she wanted her to help with her precious glass. 'Are you sure? I'm hardly going to be able to decide what you want to keep.'

'Oh, I'll decide what to keep,' she said, handing over a bundle of tissue. 'You can wrap.'

Tina smiled in spite of herself, liking her mother's succinct and pointed delineation of their duties.

And because it wasn't as if she didn't have time on her hands and because maybe it would offer them a chance to talk, maybe even to get to know each other a little better than they did, she agreed. 'You're on.'

Two hours later they'd barely made a dent on the collection and there was still precious little in the 'sell' box. Lily gave a sigh of contentment as if she'd just cleared an entire room when all they'd touched was a couple of side tables. 'Well, I think that's more than enough for the day.'

Tina looked around at what was left. At this rate it would take six months to clear the room, and then there was still the rest of the palazzo.

'Oh no,' her mother said, passing an ornament across. 'This one can go.'

Tina took it from her, a strange shivery sensation zipping out along her nerve endings. It was a prancing horse, just like the one the glassmaker had made at the factory. 'Luca took me to Murano this morning,' she said, holding the horse up to the light. 'They made one of these there while we watched.'

'I suspect that's probably where it came from. You might as well throw that one away. Nobody will buy it. They're a dime a dozen.'

Tina held the fragile glass horse. Thought of the boy with big brown eyes. Thought of another child who would have grown up with horses on the property, who would have ridden before he could walk, who would never get the chance to have his own horse.

Her son should have his own horse.

He deserved it.

'Can I have it?'

'Of course you can have it. But I thought you didn't like glass.'

'Not for me,' she said, already wrapping it carefully in layers of tissue. 'It's for…a friend.'

Carmela appeared, brandishing a tray with drinks for them both, and it was only then, thinking about the trip out to Murano, that she remembered what she had meant to tell her mother. And what she most wanted to ask. 'Oh, I meant to say, Luca's cousin asked him to drop off some flowers on the way home from Murano at Isola di San Michele. I took the opportunity to pay my respects to Eduardo.'

'Oh poor Eduardo,' Lily said on a sigh, looking wistfully out of the window. 'I do wish he hadn't left me like he did. None of this would be happening if he was still around.'

'Do you miss him?'

'Of course I do.' Lily sounded almost offended. 'Besides which, it's such a difficult business trying to find a new husband at my age. It's not easy when you're over fifty.'

She turned to her daughter. 'And that's why you should take your chances while you have them. You're young and pretty now, but it won't last, let me tell you.'

In spite of herself, Tina smiled. 'The World According to Lily' would make a fabulous book if her mother ever thought to write it. It wouldn't be a thick book, certainly, but part fashion advice, part self-help, with a big dollop of how to marry into money, and all put together by someone who had lived by its principles and—mostly—prospered, it would be a guaranteed bestseller.

But just right now she didn't want her mother's advice. What she wanted was her knowledge to answer a question that had been burning away in the back of her mind ever since her visit to the cemetery island.

'I visited the crypt, of course. I couldn't help but notice Luca's parents were both dead. I had no idea and he didn't seem to want to talk about it. What happened to them?' she ventured cautiously. 'Do you know?'

Lily sipped her gin, looking thoughtful. 'That was way before my time. Must be twenty years ago now. Maybe more. Some kind of boating accident here on the lagoon if I remember rightly. It was the reason Luca came to live with him and Agnetha, of course.'

Tina's ears pricked up. 'He lived with Eduardo? Here?'

'He grew up with them. Of course he lived here, although he'd already moved on by the time we married. I'm sure Eduardo told me. Let me see…' She hesitated a while, blinking into the distance. 'From what I remember him saying, Matteo's family offered to take him in but because Eduardo and Agnetha had no children of their own, it was decided he should go to them.'

Tina drank in the details, holes in her knowledge filling with new information. Holes filling with even more questions.

So this had been his home then.

Where he had lived with his uncle and aunt before his aunt had died and before Lily had come along…

Was that why he seemed to resent Lily so much? Because by marrying Eduardo she had stolen his inheritance out from underneath him?

Was that the reason he was so desperate to get it back?

Where the hell was she?

Luca stood at the balcony overlooking the Grand Canal wondering where she'd disappeared to. Sure, they'd had an argument, but they had a deal. One month she'd agreed to and she'd been the one to set the term. He'd checked her wardrobe. The clothes seemed untouched, her pack still there stowed in one corner. So she hadn't just decided to take advantage of his absence and renege on their deal.

So where the hell was she?

Sightseeing?

Or just blowing off steam?

He looked out over the canal that was the lifeblood of Venice, feeling sick to his stomach and desperately scanning the faces on every passing vaporetto, searching for a glimpse of Australian sunshine in a size-eight package. She was out there somewhere. She had to be.

But where?

It wasn't an excuse for the way he'd behaved, Tina thought, as she hurried along the shadowed *calles*, even if it helped explain his actions. But it still didn't excuse them. To go the lengths he had gone to get back a house simply because in other circumstances it might one day have been his—it made no sense.

Lamps were coming on around her. She looked up at the darkening sky, thinking that she'd stayed much longer at her mother's than she'd intended to, so arriving back at Luca's palazzo much later than she'd expected, the tiny horse tucked safe and sound in a stiff shopping bag Carmela had found for her.

She buzzed the bell on the gate and it clicked open, and it wasn't Aldo who greeted her at the door, but Luca.

She swallowed. After the bitter way they'd parted earlier, she wasn't sure how happy he'd be to see her.

And after what she'd learned about him, she wasn't sure she knew what to say. He saved her from having to decide.

'Have you been shopping?' he asked, looking at the bag in her hand, and after the way they'd parted she couldn't help but notice a tense note in his voice; couldn't help but feel a tinge of resentment that there would be something wrong if she had gone shopping. 'Aldo said you've been gone for hours.'

'No.' She started working herself up into righteous indignation. 'As it happens, I've been helping Lily pack some things. I didn't realise I was expected to ask for permis—'

'You were at your mother's the whole time?'

She blinked up at him. 'Do I know another Lily in Venice?'

He regarded her through eyes half-shuttered, assessing. 'You surprise me, Valentina. You constantly surprise me. You seemed so vehemently opposed to meeting with your mother.'

'I don't know why you should be so surprised,' she said, hitching up her chin as she made a move to walk past him. 'We're practically strangers. You don't know the first thing about me.'

'Don't I?' he asked, lashing out a hand to encircle her wrist, blocking off her path with the subtle shift of his body, a body built for sex, the subtle movement enough to remind her of all the heated moves it was capable of. 'And yet I know how to make the lights in your eyes explode like fireworks. I know how to turn you molten with one flick of my tongue. I know what you like and I'm thinking that's probably slightly more than the first thing about you, wouldn't you agree, Valentina?'

He was so intense. Too intense, the way his words worked in concert with his eyes, getting under her skin and worming their way into her very bones. She could scarcely breathe in his presence, so focused was his gaze upon her, the fingers wrapped around her wrist so tightly clenched.

'You can call me Tina, you know,' she whispered, desperately needing a change of subject, her words almost crackling in the heated air of his proximity. 'You don't have to do the whole Valentina thing every time. Tina works for me just fine.'

He blinked. Slowly. Purposefully. 'Why would I call you something short and sharp, when your full name is so lush and sensual? When your full name holds as many seductive hills and valleys as your perfect body?'

She couldn't answer. There were no words to answer. Not when instead of counteracting his intensity, she had inadvertently ramped it up tenfold.

'No,' he stated, with an air of authority that both infuriated her and rocked her to the soles of her feet as he pulled her close for his kiss, 'Tina does not work for me at all.'

They dined in that night, but only after they'd made love late into the night. She couldn't tell whether it was anger or relief that tinged his love-making but, whatever it was, it gave yet another nuance to the act of sex. Worst of all, it gave her reason for not hating the fact she had to be here.

Later, when still she couldn't sleep worrying about it, she slipped from the bed to stand in the big *salone* and look out through the set of four windows overlooking the Grand Canal, watching the reflection of light onto water.

Watching the seemingly endless activity of a water-borne society while her mind wandered and wondered.

What was happening to her?

She'd spent one night with him three years ago and she hadn't seen him since. After what had happened, she hadn't wanted to see him again. But sex with Luca was like an addiction that had been suppressed, a drug refused, and one taste had sent her back to that feverish place where need was paramount and hunger would not be denied.

And maybe, if she was honest with herself, she hadn't lived those three years at all.

Maybe she'd only existed in the shadow of one perfect night, one perfect night that had all too rapidly turned toxic.

Maybe she'd only barely survived.

Despite her misgivings, they seemed to slip into a routine after that. Tina would go and help her mother sort her belongings in preparation for the upcoming move. Some days Lily would be more receptive to her help than others, but she felt that finally they were building some kind of fragile rapport as they worked room by room through the maze of glass.

She still couldn't forgive her mother entirely for landing her in Luca's bed, but neither could she honestly say she wasn't enjoying the experience—at least a little.

Well, maybe more than just a little.

There was something about being with Luca that made her feel alive and sexy, vibrant and feminine, and all at the same time. It was no hardship to be seen on his arm, to feel the envy from other women, envy she enjoyed all the more because she knew it would be short-lived. It was no hardship to feel his heated glances and know what was on his mind.

And the sex was good too.

Just sex, she'd remind herself, putting the lid back on that imaginary box and tucking it under the bed when Luca went to work in the mornings.

Just sex. And in a few short weeks she would return home and it would all be a distant memory. Why shouldn't she enjoy it while it lasted?

A week after she'd arrived in Venice, she turned up at her mother's house. She heard Lily the moment she entered the rapidly emptying palazzo. The echoing torrent of French coming from upstairs almost had her turning her back and fleeing, until she realised from the few impassioned words she could understand that it wasn't fury her mother was radiating, but delight.

'What's going on?' she asked Carmela, peering suspiciously up the stairs as she peeled off her jacket.

The housekeeper took it to slide over a hanger. 'She's talking to the gallery owner, the one who has agreed to take her glass on consignment. There must be good news.'

Lily came bounding down the stairs a minute later, her eyes bright, looking more like a schoolgirl than a fifty-something woman. But then she'd changed her hair too, Tina realised, so that now it framed her face more softly, stripping years from her face.

'What is it?' Tina asked.

'You'll never guess. Antonio has a contact in London. They're doing a display of Venetian glass and they want everything I can send. Antonio thinks it will make a fortune!'

'Antonio?'

Her mother actually looked coy, her hands tangling in front of her. 'Signore Brunelli, of course, from the gallery handling the sale.'

Tina glanced across at the housekeeper, who gave a

quick nod before bustling back in to pack up the last of the kitchen, and suddenly her mother's change of mood in the last few days made some kind of sense.

And even though that was what her mother did, finding her next partner with unerring precision, Tina couldn't help but smile at seeing her so happy. 'That's great, Lily.'

'That's not all,' her mother continued, her eyes sparkling. 'He wants me to come to London with him. He says I will be the bridge between the Venetian and the British, unifying the collection and giving it purpose. He's taking me to dinner tonight to talk about the details. He thinks we should be there for a month at least.'

She took a deep breath, looking around her as if trying to work out what she'd been up to before the call. 'Well, I guess we should get to work. It will be such a relief when it's all done.'

Relief? The one hundred and eighty degree change in her mother's mood from when she'd first arrived in Venice would be something worth celebrating if only Tina wasn't left with a bad taste in her mouth. Where was her relief? Where was her upside?

She'd been the one to make the sacrifice here—forced to spend a month with a man she hated while her mother not only got on with her life but prospered. Where was the justice?

'Don't you mind about the move any more? When I came here, you were so angry with Luca, with me, with your situation—with everything! How can you be so happy now?'

'Don't you want me to be happy?' There were shades of the Lily of old in her question, shades of indignation that once would have been the spark set to combust into something more.

'Of course I do, Lily. It's just that—' She threw her

hands out wide in frustration. 'It's just that I'm still stuck with Luca while you seem to be getting on with your life now as if this is nothing but a minor inconvenience.'

'Oh, Valentina.' Her mother nodded on a sigh. 'Please don't be angry with me. Sit down a moment.' She pulled her down alongside her on a sofa. 'I have something I should say to you—Carmela will tell me off if I don't.'

She frowned. The idea of Carmela reprimanding her mother was too delicious. 'What is it?'

Lily shook her head and took her daughter's hand. 'I know we haven't always been close, but I do know I treated you appallingly when you arrived. Even before you arrived. But I was so scared,' she implored, 'don't you see? I had nobody else to turn to and Luca was threatening to throw me out onto the streets and I believed him. I had no idea he would come up with the apartment—he never hinted. I believed he would do his worst.'

Tina nodded. 'I know.' And it was good to be reminded of how afraid they'd both been; of how Luca had ruthlessly manipulated them both to get what he wanted. It was such a short time ago and yet just lately it had been so much harder to remember. 'It's okay.'

'No,' she said. 'Don't say anything. This is hard for me and you have to listen. I'm sorry I haven't been a better mother to you. I'm sorry I got you involved in all my mess. But please don't begrudge me this slice of happiness. It's been so long since I felt this way about a man.'

'I'm happy for you, Lily, truly I am. But please be careful. You've only just met the man, surely?'

Her mother smiled and shrugged, looking into the middle distance as if she was seeing something that Tina couldn't. 'Sometimes that's all it takes. Little more than a heartbeat and you know that he's the one.'

'Is that how you felt with Dad, then? And Eduardo and Hans and Henri-Claude?'

Lily dropped her head and sighed. 'No. I'm ashamed to say it's not. I'm not proud of my track record, but this time it's the real thing, Valentina. I know it. And what I want for you is to know this same happiness. Is there no chance that you and Luca—'

Tina stood, unable to sit, needing to move. 'No. None.'

'Are you sure? Has he said nothing about staying?'

'Of course I'm sure, and no he hasn't. Because he won't. He's not a man to change his mind, Lily, and I don't want him to. In fact, I can't wait for this month to be over. I can't wait to get home and see Dad again.'

'Oh. I see. It's a shame, though. Especially after what you've been through, losing his baby and everything. Surely he realises he risks putting you through all that again.'

'He doesn't know!' she said, wishing to God she'd never told her mother about her baby. 'And he won't know. There's no point in him knowing. It's…history.'

'But surely it's his history too.'

'It's too late for that,' she said, running her hands through her hair and pulling her ponytail tight, pulling her fraying thoughts tight with it and plastering a smile on her face that touched nowhere near her heart. 'Now, where do we start today?'

'You didn't have to blackmail me to get my mother out of the palazzo, you know.'

Luca and Tina had made love long into the night and now they lay spooned together in that dreamy place between sex and sleep while their bodies hummed down from the heights of passion.

He pulled her closer and pressed his lips to her shoulder. 'What do you mean?'

'All you had to do was wave that gallery owner, Antonio Brunelli in front of her nose and she would have done anything you wanted in a heartbeat.'

He stilled alongside her. 'Lily and Antonio Brunelli? Is that so?'

'I suspect she already believes herself in love with him. So you see, you could have saved yourself all this trouble if you'd just introduced her to Antonio in the first place.'

He breathed out on a sigh, warm air fanning her skin. 'I never realised it would be that easy or maybe I would have.'

It irked her that she felt deflated. She shouldn't feel deflated. She hadn't wanted to be here after all. 'So maybe you should have.'

'Ah,' he said softly, cupping one breast so tenderly in his warm hand, 'but then I wouldn't have you.'

She squeezed her eyes shut, trying to sort out the tangle of her thoughts. He meant he wouldn't have her for sex, he meant. Nothing more.

It was ridiculous to imagine he meant any more than that when his intentions had always been so clear from the start.

All the same, she wished she hadn't pushed him. She wished she'd left him saying maybe he wouldn't have bothered. She wished she didn't secretly yearn for things to be different.

And she wished to hell she understood why she wanted them to be so.

CHAPTER TWELVE

TINA checked her watch and pulled her new computer onto her lap. As much as she'd protested when Luca had given it to her, she loved what it could do. Talking face to face with her father for one. It would be around eight p.m. at home now and Mitch would be finished work and hanging around the study waiting for her call. It was good to hear how everything was going on the farm. It grounded her, and made her realise how much a fantasy her life in Venice was.

They talked of the now completed shearing, which had gone better than anticipated and Tina was already calculating what the bales of wool would bring in when she heard it in the background—a female voice.

'Who's there with you, Dad? I didn't know you had company or I wouldn't have called.'

'Oh, it's just Deidre, love. By the way, when are you coming home?'

'Deidre? Deidre Turner, you mean? But surely the shearing's finished. Why's she still there?'

'She's…er…she's helping out with the cooking, just while you're away. Now, when are you coming home?'

'Oh Dad,' she said, distracted by thoughts of Deidre Turner and what might really be going on at home while she was away. Deidre was a widow, she knew, her childhood sweetheart husband of twenty years killed in a tractor accident a few years back. She'd never so much as looked at another man. Or so Tina had thought. But maybe she was looking now.

She smiled as she framed her next question. 'Are you sure you really want me home?' adding before he could answer, 'Don't worry, Dad. There's ages yet. I'll let you know when I've booked.'

'Tina, you've already been away three weeks. If you don't book a flight soon, you won't get one.'

Shock sizzled down her spine.

Three weeks?

That couldn't be right, could it? No. Surely it was more like two?

But when she looked at the calendar she saw he was right. Eight days she had left.

Eight nights.

And then she would be free to leave, her end of the bargain satisfied.

'Tina? You okay?'

She blinked and turned back to her father. 'Sorry, Dad,' she said, shaking her head. 'Of course you're right. I'll book. I'll let you know.'

She ended the call, stunned and bewildered. How could she have so lost track of time? When she'd first arrived in Venice she couldn't wait to get away. But now—when she could count the days and nights remaining on her fingers—now the thought of leaving ripped open a chasm in her gut and left her feeling empty and bereft.

One month she'd agreed to and now that month was nearly up and, as much as she looked forward to seeing her father again, the thought of leaving Venice…

Leaving Luca…

Oh God, no, she thought, don't go there. She'd always

been going to leave. She'd been the one to set that condition and Luca had agreed. He expected her to go. Clearly she was simply getting used to dressing up in beautiful clothes and living as if she belonged here. But she didn't belong here. She didn't belong with Luca. She would book her flight home and think about how good it would be to see her father again. She'd feel better once she'd booked.

She was sure she would.

'I booked my flight home today.'

Luca stilled at the cabinet where he was pouring them both a glass of sparkling prosecco. The pouring stopped. This wasn't how he'd planned tonight to go. The trinket in his pocket weighed heavy like the ball in his gut. 'So when do you go?'

'A week tomorrow. I was lucky enough to get a seat. Flights are pretty fully booked this time of year.'

Lucky.

The word stuck in his throat. Was she in such a goddamned hurry to leave? He'd thought she was enjoying their time together. She'd certainly given him that impression in bed.

And while he'd always planned to dump her, the thought that she might hang around a little longer would have meant putting off the inevitable just that bit longer too.

But now she'd booked, he'd have to bring his plans forward. A shame when she'd provided such a useful distraction from the working day.

He finished pouring his drink and turned around, handing her a glass. 'Very fortunate,' he said, raising his glass to her. 'In which case I propose a toast—to the time we have left. May we use it wisely.'

She blinked up at him as she sipped her wine, her amber eyes surprisingly flat, with less sparkle than the wine in her glass, and he wondered at that. Wondered if she'd been hoping he'd changed his mind and might ask her to stay.

He might have. But not now, not now she'd taken the initiative.

'And we might as well start tonight,' he said, putting down his glass to reach into his pocket. 'I have a surprise for you. Tonight I have tickets to the opera, and I want you to wear this…' From a black velvet box, he extracted the string of amber beads, a large amber pendant in the middle that glinted like gold as he laid it over her hand.

Her eyes grew wide. 'It's beautiful,' she said.

'The colour matches your eyes.' He turned her gently, securing the gems around her throat, turning her back around to see. He nodded. 'Perfect. As soon as I saw them, I knew they would be perfect for you. Here, there are earrings too.'

She cupped them in her hand. 'I'll take good care of them.'

He shrugged, reaching for his wine, wanting to fill this empty hole in his gut with…*something*. 'They are yours. Now, we need to leave in half an hour. It's time to get dressed.'

Luca's unexpected gift had thrown her off balance, the gems sitting fat and heavy upon her neck, weighing her down, anchoring her to a false reality.

Nothing in Venice was real, she decided, as she caught a final glimpse of herself in the floor to ceiling gilt-framed mirror. Nothing was as it seemed.

Least of all her.

In an emerald-coloured gown, the amber necklace warm and golden at her throat, she looked as if she could have stepped out of a fairy tale, a modern day princess about to be swept off to the ball with the charming prince.

As for Luca, just one glance at him in his dark Italian designer suit, all lean, powerful masculinity, waiting for her to take his arm, was enough to make her heart pound.

She'd be gone in a week.

Returned to the dusty sheep and their wide brown land.

Gone.

Why did that thought set her heart to lurch and her stomach to squeeze tight when home was where her heart was? What was happening to her?

'Ready?' he said, a kernel of concern in his dark eyes, and she smiled up at him tremulously.

'I've never been to the opera before,' she offered by way of explanation. 'Never to a live performance at a real opera house.'

'You've never seen *La Traviata* then?'

She shook her head, never more conscious of their different lives and backgrounds. 'I don't know anything about it.'

'And did you never see the film, *Moulin Rouge*?'

'I saw that, yes.'

'Then you know the story. It was based on the opera.'

'Oh,' she said, remembering, 'Then it's a sad story. It seemed so unfair that Satine should find love when it was already too late, when her time was already up.'

He shrugged, as if it was of no consequence. 'Life doesn't always come with happy endings. Come,' he said, slipping her wrap around her shoulders, 'let's go.'

The entrance to the opera house at the Scuola Grande di San Giovanni Evangelista was set inside a small square, made smaller this night by the glittering array of people who stood sipping prosecco in the evening air. Heads turned as Luca arrived, heads that took her in almost as an afterthought, heads that nodded as if to say, *She's still here then.*

Tina smiled as Luca made his way through the crowd, stopping here and there for a brief word, always accompanied by a swift and certain appraisal of the woman on his arm. It didn't bother her any more. She was getting used to the constant appraisals, the flash of cameras going off around them. She was getting used to seeing the pictures of them turning up in the newspapers attending this function or that restaurant.

What they would say when she was gone didn't matter. Except there was that tiny squeeze of her stomach again at the thought of leaving.

She would miss this fantasy lifestyle, the dressing up, being wined and dined in amazing restaurants in one of the most incredible cities in the world.

But it wasn't just that.

She would miss Luca.

Strange to think that when at first she had been desperate for the month to be over, desperate to get away. But it was true.

She would miss his dark heated gaze. She would miss the warmth of his body next to hers in bed at night, the tender way he cradled her in his arms while he slept, his breathing slow and deep.

She would miss his love-making.

For there was no point pretending it was "just sex" any longer.

No point pretending it was something she could compartmentalize and lock away in a box and shove under the bed. It was too much a part of her now. It had given her too much.

'Just sex' could never feel this good.

He led her inside the building, more than five hundred

years old and showing it, the wide marble steps to the first floor concert hall worn with the feet of the centuries, gathering in this place to listen and enjoy and celebrate music and song.

And art, she realised, looking around her.

The ceiling soared, the height of another two storeys above them, held up by massive columns of marble, the panels of the walls filled with Renaissance art featuring saints and angels and all manner of heavenly scenes, framed in gold.

Here and there the floor dipped a little, rose again as they walked; here and there a corner looked not quite square, a column not quite straight.

Unconsciously she clutched Luca's arm a little tighter as he led her to her seat, fazed by the sensation of the floor shifting beneath her feet, as if the weight of the marble was pushing the building into the marshy ground beneath.

'Is something wrong?' Luca asked beside her, picking up on her unease.

'It is safe, isn't it? The building, I mean.'

He laughed then, a low rumble of pleasure that echoed into her bones. 'The opera house has been here since the thirteenth century. I'm sure it will manage to remain standing a couple more hours.' And at the same time she realised he was laughing at her, he squeezed her hand and drew her chin to his mouth for an unexpected press of his lips. 'Do not be afraid. I assure you it is safe.'

Was it?

Breathless and giddy, she let herself be led to their seats.

Was it simply the ground shifting beneath her feet, or was it something more?

Please, God, let it be nothing more.

Heels clicked on marble floors and then stilled, the hum

of conversation dimming with the lights until finally it was time.

The music started, act one of the famous opera, and in the spacious concert hall the music soared into the heavens, giving life to the angels and the cherubs in the delicate stuccoes, taking the audience on a heavenly journey.

The singers were sublime, their voices filling the air, and it was impossible not to be carried along with the tragic story of Violetta, as she discovered the heroine was called in this original version, and her lovers, warring for the affections of the dying courtesan. And yet, through it all, she had never been more aware of Luca's heated presence at her side, at the touch of his thigh against hers, to the brush of his shoulder against hers.

She wanted to drink in that touch while she still could. She wanted to imprint it on her memory so she could take it out and remember it on the long nights ahead, when she was home and Venice and Luca was a distant memory.

The story built, the young lovers united at last, only to be forced apart by family.

She seemed more acutely aware of Luca than ever. The score was in Italian and, while she caught only a snatched phrase here and there, she understood the passion, she felt the pain and the torment.

How ironic, she thought, that he had brought her here tonight, to hear the story of a fallen woman for whom love was painful and hard won and ultimately futile.

Had he brought her here as some kind of lesson?

That life, as he had told her before they had left the palazzo, did not always have a happy ending?

The third act came to an end. Despite bursts of elation, bursts of happiness, Violetta's death had always been a tragedy waiting to happen.

She felt tears squeeze from her eyes at the finale, wondering why this story affected her so deeply. It was just a story, she told herself, just fiction. It wasn't true.

And yet she felt the tragedy of Violetta's wasted love to her core.

Why?

When in a few days, little more than a week, she would be free to return home.

Free.

There was no chance she would end up like Violetta. She wouldn't let it.

And yet, increasingly, she felt herself tipping, tripping over uneven ground, trying pointlessly to keep her balance and all the while hurtling towards that very same finale.

'What did you think?' he asked her as they rose to their feet, the audience wild, celebrating a magnificent performance. 'Did you understand it?'

And she sniffed through her tears as she nodded and clapped as hard as anyone.

More than you will ever know.

That night sleep eluded her. She lay awake listening to the sound of Luca's steady breathing, the sound of the occasional water craft passing and all overlaid by the tortured ramblings of her own mind.

In the end she gave up on sleep entirely, slipped on the jade silk gown and resumed her vigil at the windows, feeling strangely forlorn and desolate as she stared out over the wide canal, drinking in a view that would all too soon be nothing more than a fond memory.

And even though she tried to tell herself it was the opera that was to blame for her mood, she knew it was more. She knew it came from deep inside herself.

She sighed as the light curtains puffed in the breeze and floated around her. The evenings were distinctly cooler now, clouds more frequent visitors to the skies blocking the moon and sun, the wind picking up and carrying with it the scent of a summer in decline. She stood there at the open windows and drank it all in, building an album in her mind of the scents and sounds and sights that she would be able to pull out and turn the pages of when she was home.

Next week.

Anguish squeezed the air from her lungs.

Suddenly it was all too soon.

She heard a movement behind her. She heard a noise like something tearing and she made to turn her head.

'Don't turn,' he instructed.

'What are you doing?'

'What I knew I had to do when I saw you standing framed in the window,' he said, and something in his voice gave her a primitive thrill, a delicious sense of anticipation that made her turn her face back towards the darkened canal. 'Keep watching the water, and the water craft.'

'As you wish,' she said, a smile curling her lips as she felt the heat at her back as he came close and joined her on the balcony, a smile that turned distinctly to thoughts of sex when she felt him hard and ready between them. She sighed at the feel of him. God, she would miss this. She put a hand to the nearest curtain, meaning to pull it closed.

'Leave it,' he said. 'Leave the curtains. I want your hands on the balcony.'

And with a rush of sizzling realisation, his meaning became crystal clear. 'But we can't…not here…not on the balcony…with the boats.'

He dropped his mouth to the curve of her neck, kissing her skin, his teeth grazing her flesh, stoking a fire that burned much, much lower. 'Yes. Here, on the balcony. With the boats.'

She gasped. 'But—'

'Keep watching,' he said when she tried to turn, to remonstrate, but he was right behind her and she was pinned up against the cool marble balustrade, cool at her front, hot where he pressed against her back, as another craft chugged slowly by. 'They can't see us,' he said, as she felt the slide of her gown up her calves, his fingertips tickling the sensitive skin at the back of her knees, making her shiver in her secret pleasure. 'Even if anyone looks, all they will see will be shadows at a window. One shadow, where you and I join.'

The craft disappeared, the chug of its engines replaced by the slap of water against the foundations as air curled around her legs and his fingers eased the silk of her gown higher to find the cleft between her legs and slide one long finger along that sensitive seam, teasing with just a whisper of a touch, making her nerve endings scream with impatience.

'You're beautiful,' he whispered against her throat, his teeth grazing her skin, his finger delving deeper, and it was all she could do to keep her knees locked in place and not sag boneless to the balcony floor.

Unfair, she thought on a whimper as she felt herself being angled over the balustrade, felt the delicious press of his hardness at her very core, that he could do this to her, reduce her to a mass of tangled nerve endings that spoke the same message—need. Pure and simple, unadulterated need.

For she needed him inside her just as she needed the oxygen in her lungs. Needed him inside her and all around her just as she needed the sun and moon and sky.

He gave her what she needed, pressing into her in one fluid stroke that filled her in all the places that ached but one. Because there was no filling the ache in her heart.

For in a few short days she was leaving. And she couldn't bear the thought of it.

Couldn't bear the thought of leaving Luca.

God help me, she thought, as he moved inside her, taking her once again to that amazing place, a tear sliding unbidden down her cheek, but this was more than just need.

I love him.

CHAPTER THIRTEEN

HER period arrived midway through the next day and Tina couldn't suppress a bubble of disappointment. Now there was a way to celebrate their final few days together.

Not.

But there was an upside of course, she reasoned, because at least it meant that this time she wouldn't be going home with any surprises.

And why that thought didn't please her more than it did made no sense at all.

She rested her head against the bathroom mirror, feeling the familiar ache deep inside, a niggling question she'd been avoiding all the time she'd been in Venice now gnawing at her to be noticed.

Should she tell Luca about their lost baby?

It had been so easy to avoid the question at first, when she'd thought she'd never see him again. It had been easy when she'd arrived in Venice, and when mutual resentment and a deal the devil would have been proud of had been the thing that bound them together. It had been so easy to ask herself what would be the point of rehashing the past by telling him? What purpose would it serve? It wasn't as if she owed him after what he had done.

But now, after these last weeks with him, she wondered how long she could avoid telling him—that there was a headstone on a grave in Australia with his child's name on it.

How could she not tell him?

Wouldn't she want to know if their positions were reversed?

Wouldn't she have a right to know?

She peeled herself away from the bathroom mirror and drifted through the bedroom. Strange, she mused, how love could change your view on the world.

Because suddenly there were no more reasons to avoid the truth. She wanted Luca to know everything.

And even though the news would no doubt come as a shock and he would be entitled to be angry at her for not telling him earlier, she didn't want secrets between them.

Not any more.

She'd lived with this secret too long.

As for her love? Well, that would hardly be welcome news either—for had Luca once tried to talk her out of booking her flight home?

That was one secret she could keep.

Besides which, she would have more than enough trouble working out how to tell him the first.

Luca scanned the papers and swore out loud. His assistant came running. 'I thought you said you'd checked these signatures!' he yelled. 'Didn't you notice there was one missing?'

The assistant dithered and flapped and promised to fix whatever was wrong right away and Luca swept his offer aside and snatched up the papers himself. 'I'll do it!' he growled. He could do with a walk. He'd been in a hell of a mood all day and he couldn't really put his finger on why.

Yes, he could!

He didn't want her to damned well go, that was why.

She'd melted into his arms last night on the balcony as if she'd been made of honey, golden and sweet, and he'd never wanted to let her go.

But he had to. He had no choice. There was no other choice.

And in a way he was grateful for his flustered assistant for finding him something to legitimately take his anger out on, because he'd been spoiling for a fight ever since he'd left Valentina this morning.

What better reason? Because without Lily's signature in that spot on that contract, the palazzo was still legally hers, regardless of all the other papers that had been signed and countersigned. Regardless of the fact that his people had been working on the palazzo to shore it up and get it stable before the real work began. And despite the fact that she now owned the apartment lock, stock and barrel.

Maybe it was his fault for taking too much time off lately to spend with Valentina and trusting his staff to do the jobs they should, and that thought didn't make him any happier.

He needed that signature.

Carmela let him into the apartment and showed him to the *salone*, where he paced its length while he waited. He glanced at the caller ID when his cellphone rang and pressed the receive button. 'Matteo. *Sì!*'

He grunted when Matteo complimented him on the photograph of him and Valentina at the opera in the online papers this morning. He didn't want to be reminded of Valentina, even if his plan to have their romance followed by the papers and have them openly speculating about the possibilities of a new Barbarigo bride had worked supremely well. 'But that's not why I'm calling,' Matteo continued. 'I was wondering if you and Valentina would come to dinner on Friday evening.'

'*Sì*. I can make it, but Valentina will be gone by then.'

'Gone? Gone where?'

'Home.'

'A shame. So when is she coming back?'

'Never.'

'Why? I like her, very much. It's time you settled down, Luca. She seems perfect for you.'

Luca laughed. 'Forget it, Matteo, I'm not looking for a wife. Least of all someone like Valentina.' He tried to remember why. Tried to dredge up all the reasons why it had once seemed so true. Tried to bundle them all up into some kind of argument that might convince his cousin. Failed, and changed tack. 'This is sport, nothing more. Rest assured, she won't be in Venice come Friday. I'm making sure of it.'

He heard a polite cough behind him and turned. 'You wanted to see me?' Lily offered, one eyebrow arched, her fingers laced elegantly together in front of her.

He cut the call and slipped his phone into his pocket and pulled out an envelope from another. 'I have some paper-work for you to sign,' he said, wondering how much she'd heard. 'It seems you missed a signature before.'

'I spoke to Valentina yesterday,' she said, ignoring him as he placed the paper down on a nearby desk and held out a pen for her. 'Her flight is on Monday. What exactly is this "sport" you are planning?'

'Who says I was talking about Valentina? Now, if you would just sign here…'

'I heard what you said. What game are you playing, Luca?'

'Just sign the form, Lily.'

'Tell me. Because if you are planning on hurting my daughter…'

'You expect me to believe you, of all people, care? You,

who shipped her out here to bail you out of the mess you'd made of your own life? You, who would sell your daughter to the devil if it profited you?'

'Guilty,' she said, 'on all charges,' surprising him with her easy admission. 'But these last few weeks I've got to know my daughter properly, and I like her. I like her a lot, so much so that I will miss her terribly when she's gone. And I know I have no right to even ask, but I so wish she did not have to go.'

The world had gone mad! Nothing was as he had thought it would be. Nothing was how it should be. Valentina was going. He should feel happy. He would be happy. Just as soon as this black cloud lifted from his shoulders.

But Lily, he'd expected to be happy too—a new house, money, a new man—the Lily he knew should not need her daughter's presence a moment longer. And yet here she was practically despairing that she was leaving.

What the hell was happening?

'Promise me you won't hurt her, Luca,' Lily inserted into the weighted silence. 'Please promise me that.'

And the frustrations of the last twenty-four hours—the news that Valentina was leaving—a night at the opera with a woman who looked like a goddess followed by a night of exquisite love-making—the missed signature—all coalesced to form one molten rage. 'I'm not promising anything!'

'But she doesn't deserve to be hurt. She's done nothing—'

'You've got no idea what she did! This is no more than she deserves!'

And her mother grew claws before his eyes. 'Oh, I'd say it's clearly much less than she deserves, after the misery you put her through.'

'What are you talking about? I gave her the best night of her life!'

'You clearly gave her one hell of a lot more than that!'

The thump in his temples thundered out a warning that pieced together in ugly sequence in his brain. 'What do you mean? What are you saying?'

She shook her head, hand over her mouth. 'I'm sorry, I shouldn't have said that. If you don't know, then maybe there's a reason for that.'

A reason for not knowing?

Not knowing *what*?

What the hell had he given her?

Why wouldn't he be told?

Unless...

And as his blood surged loud in his ears, a drum call to war, a drum call to action, the thumping beat of his heart pounded out the only possible answer and he felt sick to his very core.

'Are you saying Valentina was pregnant—pregnant with my child?'

Lily stiffened where she stood, but her eyes were wide and fearful, the fingers of one hand clutching at her throat. 'I didn't tell you that.'

He turned, already on his way out. Already with one mission in mind.

'Luca—wait! Listen to me!'

But there was no waiting. No listening. Because for three weeks he had harboured this woman in his house, treated her like a princess, made love to her like she actually meant something, and all the time she had been harbouring the ugliest of secrets.

Had she been laughing all this time? At him not knowing? At him, thinking he had the upper hand when all the while she'd already exacted her revenge in the worst possible way?

Now it was time to find out the truth.

The truth about what she had done to his child!

CHAPTER FOURTEEN

HE FOUND her curled into a window seat tapping away on the laptop, her hair hanging loose, the ends flicking free around her face, and wearing *gelato*-coloured clothes, looking like innocence personified.

Innocence?

Oh no.

He felt like growling.

Once he might have been taken in. But not now.

Because now he knew better.

She looked up as he approached and an electric smile like he hadn't seen before lit up her face for just a moment, until she blinked and the smile turned to a frown. The laptop got forgotten on a cushion beside her as she sat up. 'What's wrong, Luca? Why are you home so early?'

'All this time…' He dragged in air, needing the time and the space to get the words out in the order he wanted when so many were queued up ready and willing to be fired off. 'All this time, I never imagined you were capable of such a thing.' He shook his head from side to side as he looked at her, seeing a new Valentina where once he had seen a goddess, seeing finally the spiteful, vengeful bitch that she really was. 'When were you planning on telling me? Or was it your dirty little secret?'

The blood drained from her face, guilt leaching her

face. 'Luca?' And from where he was standing the pathetic whimper of his name on her lips sounded like a confession.

He shook his head, blood pounding in his temples, pounding out a call to war, the sound stealing the volume from his voice until his words came out rasping against the air. 'You don't even try to deny it!'

Her hand plastered over her mouth. More denial. *More proof.*

'Luca,' she implored from behind her hand as the tears started to fall. He was unmoved. Of course there would be tears. He'd expected them. Because she had been found out for what she really was.

'How long,' he demanded, 'were you going to keep it a secret?'

'Who told you?' she asked. 'Was it Lily?'

And her words damned her to a hell worse than anything he could devise. He felt sickened by her confession. Sickened that the denial he hadn't realised he'd been secretly hoping for did not materialise.

Sickened that she could have done such a thing.

'Does it matter?' He strode away, unable to look at her for a moment longer, clawing fingers through his hair until his scalp burned with the pain. And still it wasn't enough. Then he spun back. 'Why didn't you tell me?'

She looked as if she'd lost her place in the world.

She looked as if she was wondering what had gone wrong.

She looked as guilty as hell.

'I was going to!'

'Like hell!'

'I was!' And then she was up from the couch, clutching at his arm. 'Luca, you have to believe me, I was going to tell you. I know I hadn't before, but I decided this morning that you should know.'

'This morning! How convenient! What a shame someone else got there first.' He brushed her hand away. 'I don't want anyone like you touching me. Not after what you've done.'

She blinked up at him, all big golden *fake* eyes. 'But you wouldn't have wanted to know, surely? You wouldn't have wanted to know I was pregnant, not after the way we'd parted.'

He looked down at her with all the hate in the world on his face. 'I might at least have wanted a say in how our baby met its end. Don't you think I was entitled to at least that much?'

Tina stopped and stared, sideswiped by the ugliness of his words. She'd been defending one charge—that she had never told him about their child, a charge she'd known would be difficult enough. But suddenly the argument, like the ground beneath her, had shifted again and Luca was accusing her of…what?

'What are you saying? What exactly are you accusing me of?'

'Don't pretend you don't know! Because you know what you did. You murdered my child!'

The clocks stopped, while the magnitude—the sheer injustice—of his allegation rolled over her like waves upon a beach, dumping her head first into the sand, only to come up barely alive, barely breathing.

'No,' she muttered, from that vague, shell-shocked place she was. 'No, that's not how it was.'

'You as much as admitted it!'

'No! Our baby died.'

'Because you made it happen!'

'No! I did nothing! I know I didn't tell you about our baby, but I did nothing—'

'I don't believe you, Valentina. I wish I did, but you

damned yourself when you pretended you were going to tell me today. You never made any effort to tell me. You were never going to tell me.'

'Luca, listen to me, you've got it all wrong.'

'Have I? I curse myself for taking a woman like you back into my bed, knowing now what you did that first time. Knowing what you might be capable of again.'

'I had a miscarriage! Our baby died and it was nothing to do with me. Why won't you listen to me?'

'A miscarriage? Is that what they call it where you come from?'

'Luca, don't be like this. Please don't be like this. I could never do such a thing!'

But dark eyes bore coldly down upon her, judge, jury and executioner in two deep fathomless holes. 'Then why did you?'

And she knew there was only one card left to play.

'I love you,' she said, hoping to reach some part of him, hoping to appeal to whatever scrap of his heart might hear her pleas. Might believe her.

She didn't know how he would respond. Disbelief. Horror. Indifference. She braced herself for the worst.

But the worst was nothing she could have imagined. He laughed. He threw back his head and laughed, and the sound rang out through the palazzo, filling the high-ceilinged room, reverberating off the walls. A mad sound. A sound that scared her.

'Perfect,' he said, when the fit had passed. 'That's just perfect.'

'Luca? I don't understand. Why is that so funny?'

'Because you were supposed to fall in love with me. Don't you see? That was all part of the plan.'

Ice ran down her spine, turning her rigid. 'Plan? What plan?'

'You still can't work it out? Why do you think I asked you here?'

'To pay off my mother's debt. On my back. In your bed.' The words came out all twisted and tight, but that was how she felt, like a mop squeezed and wrung out and left out to dry in a twisted, tangled mess.

'But it wasn't only her debt,' he said in a half snarl. 'It was your debt too. Because nobody walks out on me. Not the way you did. Not ever.'

'All of this because I slapped you and walked out?' She was incredulous. 'You went to all this trouble to settle the score?'

'Believe me, it was no trouble given Lily's predilection for spending.'

'So why,' she asked, her hands fisting, her throat thick, but damn him to hell and back, she refused to give in to the urge to cry, not before she knew all of the awful truth, 'why did you want me to fall in love with you? Why was that part of your so-called plan?'

'Oh,' he said, 'that's the best bit. 'Because once you fell in love with me, it would make dumping you so much more satisfying.'

'But why, when I was leaving anyway?'

'Do you think I was planning to wait until your flight to cut you loose? Not a chance. And now, after finding out the kind of person you really are, I'm glad to see the back of you.' He dragged in air. 'What a fool I was. To think I let you back into my life after what you'd done. What were you hoping this time? To do it all again? To go home with another child in your belly—another child on whom you could exact your own ugly revenge?'

She blinked against the wall of hatred directed her way, as his words flayed her like no whip ever could. They scored her and stung her and ripped at her psyche.

And there was nothing she could say or do, nothing but feel the weight of her futile love for this man sucking her down into the depths of one of Venice's canals. Knowing there would be no rescue.

'I'll go, Luca. You clearly want me gone and I don't want to stay so I'll pack up and leave now and consider myself duly dumped.'

She walked to the door, holding her head, if not her heart, high. And then she turned. 'There's one more thing I should have told you about our baby. Add it to my list of crimes if you must, I don't care. I named him Leo.'

He wandered the palazzo like a caged lion. He felt like a caged lion. He wandered through his bedroom, he wandered past the windows where they'd made love, he wandered out of his home and out through the *calles* of Venice, past the scaffolding around Eduardo's old palazzo, where the engineers and builders were already hard at work shoring up the foundations, and back again and still he couldn't get her out of his mind.

Still she was gone.

But he'd got what he wanted, hadn't he? He still wanted her gone, given what she had done.

He'd got what he had wanted all along. He'd got rid of her. He'd got even.

So why the hell wasn't he happy now she was gone?

Why was he so miserable now she was gone?

Damn the woman! He'd almost wanted her to stay. He'd almost figured she'd meant something to him before her betrayal. He'd almost factored in a measure of longevity before he'd learned the truth about what she really was. He didn't want to think about the kind of person she really was.

He got back to his study and looked at the file someone had placed on his desk while he'd been away. A file he'd asked for. A file that bore a name tag he wasn't sure he entirely recognised.

Leo Henderson Barbarigo.

Why did that name send shivers down his spine? And then he opened the file and read and realised why he'd felt so sick all this time.

Because it was true that mad in that night of love-making that he and Valentina had conceived a child.

A son.

Because it was true that the child had been lost.

Their son.

But not because Valentina had brought an end to that pregnancy, as he'd so wrongly accused her of.

Valentina had been speaking the truth.

Oh God, what had he done?

Suddenly all the injustice in the world swirled and spun like threads and blame and hope all intermingled and tangled.

And he hoped to God it was not too late to do something to make up for it.

CHAPTER FIFTEEN

LUCA had figured a chartered jet should give him a fighting chance of catching her given a commercial flight's connections along the route. A chartered jet, a fast car and a GPS set for somewhere called Junee, New South Wales—with any luck he'd be right behind her.

So when he arrived at the gate marked 'Magpie Springs' and rattled the car across the cattle grid, he thought he'd done it, that soon he would see her. That soon he would have a chance to make up for it all.

He followed the bumpy dirt track, sheep scattering in his path and increasingly wondering where the hell any house might be and if he'd taken a wrong turn, when he rounded a bend and there was the house, nestled under a stand of old shade trees.

He pulled the BMW to a stop, sending up a cloud of dust that floated on the air. He climbed from the car, never more acutely aware of the expanse of blue sky than at this far-flung end of the world, and an October that felt more like April to him, with its promise of coming heat rather than a final farewell in the sun's rays.

A screen door opened and a man emerged, letting the door slam shut behind him. Tall, rangy and sun-drenched, he stopped to assess the new arrival, his eyes missing nothing. *Her father*, he guessed, and felt himself stand taller under his scrutiny.

'*Signore*—Mr Henderson?'

'Are you that Luca fella my Tina's been talking about?'

He felt an unfamiliar stab of insecurity. *What had she told him?*

'I am he,' he said, introducing himself properly as he held out his hand.

The other man regarded it solemnly for just a moment longer than Luca would have liked, before taking it in his, a work-callused hand, the skin of his forearm darker even than Luca's, but with a distinct line where his tan ended where his shirt sleeve ended between shoulder and elbow.

'I'm here to see Valentina.'

The older man regarded him levelly, giving him the opportunity to find the resemblance, finding it in a place that made the connection unmistakable—in his amber eyes—darker than Valentina's, almost caramel, but her eyes nonetheless.

'Even if I wanted to let you see her,' he started in his lazy drawl, and Luca felt a mental, *male*!, 'she's not here. You've missed her.'

Panic squeezed Luca's lungs. He'd been so desperate to track her home to Australia, he'd never thought for a moment she'd take off for somewhere else. 'Where has she gone?'

Her father thought about that for a moment and Luca felt as if he were being slowly tortured. 'Sydney,' he finally said. 'A couple of hours ago. But she wouldn't tell me where or why. Only that it was important.'

Luca knew where and he had a pretty good idea why.

'I have to find her,' he said, already turning for the car. If she was two hours ahead he could still miss her…

'Before you go…' he heard behind him.

'Yes?'

'Tina was bloody miserable when she came home. I only let her get on that bus because she insisted.' He hesitated a moment there, letting the tension draw out. 'Just don't send her home any more miserable, all right?'

Luca nodded, understanding. There was an implicit threat in his words, a threat that told him that this time was for keeps. 'I can't guarantee anything, but I will do my best.' And then, because he owed it to the man who had been prepared to put his own property on the line to bail out a sinking Lily, even when there was no way he could, 'I love your daughter, Signore Henderson,' he said, astounding himself by the truth of it. 'I want to marry her.'

'Is that so?' her father said, scratching his whiskered chin. 'Then let's hope, if you find her, that that's what she wants too.'

The cemetery sat high on a hill leading down to a cliff top overlooking a cerulean sea that stretched from the horizon and crashed to foaming white on the cliff face below. The waves were wild today, smashing against the rocks and turning to spray that flew high on a wind that gusted and whipped at her hair and clothes.

Tina turned her face into the spray as another wave boomed onto the rocks below, and drank in the scent of air and sea and salt. She'd always loved it here, ever since her father had brought her here as a child for their seaside holiday and he'd wondered at the endless sea while they'd wandered along the cliff-top path.

They'd come across the cemetery back then, wandering its endless pathways and reading the history of the region in its gravestones. Then it had been a fascination, now it was something more than just a cemetery with a view, she thought, reminded of another time, another cemetery, that one with a stunning view of Venice through its tall iron gates.

She wandered along a pathway between old graves with stones leaning at an angle or covered in lichen towards a newer section of the cemetery, where stones were brighter, the flowers fresher.

She found it there and felt the same tug of disbelief—the same pang of pain—she felt whenever she saw it, the simple heart-shaped stone beneath which her tiny child was buried, the simple iron lace-work around the perimeter.

She knelt down to the sound of the cry of gulls and the crash of waves against the cliffs. 'Hello, Leo,' she said softly. 'It's Mummy.' Her voice cracked on the word and she had to stop and take a deep breath before she could continue. 'I've brought you a present.'

Bubble wrap gave way to tissue paper as she carefully unwrapped the tiny gift. 'It's a horse,' she said, holding the glass up to the sunlight to check it for fingerprints. 'All the way from Venice. I saw a man make one from a fistful of sand.'

She placed it softly in the lawn at the base of the simple stone. 'Oh, you should have seen it, Leo, it was magical, the way he turned the rod and shaped the glass. It was so clever, and I thought how much you would have enjoyed it. And I thought how you should have such a horse yourself.'

He watched her from a distance, wanting to call out to her with relief before she disappeared again, but he saw her kneel down and he knew why.

His son's grave.

Something yawned open inside him, a chasm so big and empty he could not contemplate how it could ever be filled.

From his vantage point, he saw her lips move, saw her work something in her hands, saw the glint of sunlight on glass and felt the hiss of his breath through his teeth—heard the crunch of gravel underfoot as his feet moved forward of their own accord.

She heard it too, ignored it for a second and then glanced his way, glanced again, her eyes widening in shock, her face bleaching white when she realised who it was.

'Hello, Valentina,' he said, his voice thick with emotion. 'I've come to meet my son.'

She didn't reply, whether from the shock of his sudden appearance or because there was nothing to say. He looked down at the stone, at its simple words.

Leo Henderson Barbarigo, it read, together with a date and, beneath it, the words: *Another angel in heaven.*

And even though he'd known, even though it had made his job easier to find the grave, it still staggered him. 'You gave him my name.'

'He's your son too.'

His son.

And he fell to his knees and felt the tears fall for all that had been lost.

She let him cry. She said nothing, did nothing, but when finally he looked up, he saw the tracks of her own tears down her cheeks.

'Why didn't you tell me?' The words were anguished, wrenched from a place deep inside him, but still loaded with accusation. 'Why didn't you tell me?'

She didn't flinch from his charges. 'I was going to,' she said, her voice tight, 'when our child was born. I was going to let you know you were a father.' Sadly she shook her head. 'Then there didn't seem any point.' She shrugged helplessly and he could see her pain in the awkward movement. And in this moment, under the weight of his guilt, he felt just as awkward.

'In Venice,' he started, 'I said some dreadful things. I accused you of dreadful deeds.'

'It was a shock. You didn't know.'

'Please, Valentina, do not feel you must make excuses for me. I didn't listen. You tried to tell me and I didn't listen. I didn't want to listen. It was unforgivable of me.' He shook his head. 'But now, knowing that he was stolen from us before his time, can you tell me the rest? Can you tell me what happened?'

She blinked and looked heavenwards, swiping at her cheek with the fingers of one hand. 'There's not a lot to tell. Everything was going to plan. Everything was as it should be. But at twenty weeks, the pains started. I thought that it must have been something I'd eaten, some kind of food poisoning, that it would go away. But it got worse and worse and then I started to bleed and I was so afraid. The doctors did everything they could, but our baby was coming and they couldn't stop it.' She squeezed her hands into balls in her lap, squeezed her eyes shut so hard he could feel her pain. 'Nothing they did could stop it.'

'Valentina...'

'And it hurt so much, so much more than it should, for the doctors and midwives there too, because everyone knew there was nothing they could do to save him. He was too early. Too tiny, even though his heart was beating and he was breathing and his eyes blinked open and looked up at me.'

She smiled up at him then, her eyes spilling over with tears. 'He was beautiful, Luca, you should have seen him. His skin was almost translucent, and his tiny hand wrapped around my little finger, trying to hold on.'

Her smile faded. 'But he couldn't hold on. Not for long. And all I could do was cuddle our baby while his breathing slowed and slowed until he took one final, brave little breath…'

Oh God, he thought. Their baby had died in her arms after he had been born.

Oh God.

'Who was with you?' he whispered, thinking it should have been him. 'Your father? Lily? A friend?'

She shook her head and whispered, 'No one.'

And through the rising bubble of injustice he felt at the thought that she had been alone, he thought of the man on the farm who had no idea why his daughter had suddenly rushed off to Sydney barely a moment after she'd arrived. 'Your father didn't know?'

'I couldn't bear to tell him. I was so ashamed when I found out I was pregnant. I couldn't bear to admit that I, the product of a one-night stand, had turned around and made the same mistake my parents had. So I went back to university and hid and pretended it wasn't happening. And afterwards…well, afterwards…I couldn't bear to think about it, let alone tell anyone else.' She looked up at him with plaintive eyes. 'Do you understand? Can you try to understand?'

'You should have told me. I should have been there. You should not have been alone.'

She gave a laugh that sounded more like a hiccup. 'Because you would have so welcomed that call, to tell you I was pregnant, that you would have rushed to be by my side.' She shook her head. 'I don't think so.'

And he hated her words but he knew what she said was true.

'No,' she continued, 'I would have told you. Once the baby was born. But my parents married because of me, and look how that turned out, and I didn't want to be forced into something I didn't want, and I didn't want you to think you were being forced into something you didn't want.'

'You said that,' he said, remembering that night in Venice when she had so vehemently stated that a baby was no reason for marriage. 'So you waited.'

She nodded and swallowed, her chin kicking high into the stiff wind. 'Well, maybe…maybe also in part because I was in no hurry to see you again anyway after the way we had parted. But I knew I would have to tell you once he was born.' She stopped and breathed deep as she looked down at the tiny grave framed in iron lace. 'But when he came too early…when Leo died…I thought that would be the end of it. That there was no point…'

She shook her head, the ends of her hair whipped like a halo around her head as she looked across at him, the pain of loss etched deep in her amber eyes. 'But it wasn't. And I'm sorry you had to find out the way you did. I'm so sorry. Everything I've done seems to have turned out badly.'

'No,' he said with a sigh, gazing down at her while another set of waves crashed into the rocks behind, almost drowning his voice in the roar. 'I believe that's my territory.'

She blinked over watery eyes, confusion warring with the pain of loss.

'Come,' he said, tugging her by her hand to her feet. 'Come and walk with me a while. I need to talk to you and I'm not sure Leo would want to hear it.'

With the merest nod of her head, she let him lead her down through the cemetery, to where the cliff walk widened into a viewing platform that clung to the edge of the world and where the teeming surf smashed against the rocks with a booming roar.

She blinked into the wind, half wondering if she was dreaming, if she'd imagined him here with the power of her grief, but no, just a glance sideways confirmed it was no dream. He stood solid alongside her, his face so stern as he gazed over the edge of the continent, it could have been carved out of the stone wall of the cliffs.

It was good to see him again.

It was good he'd come to meet his son.

It hurt that he hadn't said he'd come to see her but it was good he had come. One final chance to clear the air surrounding their baby's brief existence.

Maybe now they could both move on.

Maybe.

They stood together in a silence of their own thoughts all framed by the roar and crash of water while Luca wondered where to begin. There was so much he had to explain, so much to make up for. The spray was refreshing against his skin, salty like his tears, but cleansing too. Strange he should think that, when he couldn't remember the last time he'd cried.

And with a crunching of gears inside his boarded up heart, he did.

When the news had come of his parents' deaths that foggy night when their water taxi had crashed into a craft with a broken light.

So many years ago and yet the pain felt so raw, unleashed by whatever had unlocked his heart.

Whoever had unlocked his heart.

Valentina.

He watched the waves roll in, in endless repetition. Only to be smashed to pieces against a wall of rock so hard the sea seemed to be fighting a losing battle.

Except it wasn't. Here and there boulders had fallen free, or whole sections of cliff had collapsed into the sea, undercut, worn away and otherwise toppled by the relentless force of the water.

Today he felt like that cliff, the seemingly indestructible stone no match for the constant work of time and tide. No match for a greater force.

He turned to that greater force now, a force that had been able to come back from holding her dying child in her arms to confront that child's father and seemingly accede to his demands, all the time working away on him while he crumbled before her.

And suddenly he knew what he had to say. 'Valentina,' he said, taking her hands in his, cold hands he wanted to hold and warm for ever, 'I have wronged you in so many ways.'

She smiled and he, who deserved no smile and certainly none from this woman, thought his newly exposed heart would break. 'I'm glad you came to see Leo.' He noted that she didn't dispute the fact that he'd wronged her. But there was no disputing it. He knew that now.

'I came to see you too,' he said, and her eyes widened in response, 'to see if you might understand just a little of why I acted as I did, even if those actions are unforgivable. I know I could not hope for your forgiveness, but maybe a little understanding?' He shrugged. 'When I was a child,' he started, 'my parents were both killed in a boating accident. You saw their tombs.' She nodded. 'Eduardo and Agnethe took me in, gave me a home. I went to them with nothing. My father had just invested everything he had in a start-up company he would be a key part in. With his death, it folded and all but a pittance was lost.'

'I understand,' she said. 'Lily told me you had lived with Eduardo as a child. You must have felt that when Eduardo married Lily that you lost your inheritance a second time around. No wonder you wanted the palazzo back so desperately.'

He laughed a little at that. 'Is that what you think? I

think I was too young to worry about any lost fortune back when my parents died. But it would have been useful later. I did worry about Eduardo and the palazzo. He was one of Venice's grand old men, but no businessman, living on his family's reputation while his fortune dwindled.

'I knew as I grew older that the palazzo needed major structural work, but there was never the money and when Agnethe died Eduardo missed her dreadfully and I think he forgot to care.

'I promised him then that I would pay him and Agnethe back for taking me in, by fixing the palazzo and restoring it to its former glory. I studied and I worked day and night to make it happen.'

'And then he went and married Lily.'

He smiled thinly at that. 'You could put it that way. She refused to consider my plans to restore the palazzo, she made short work of the limited funds Eduardo had at his disposal.'

Tina nodded, the strands of her hair catching on her lashes in the wind, and he ached to brush them away, but it was too soon, he knew. It was enough that she let him hold her hands. It was enough that she did not protest at the circles his thumbs made on her skin. 'That does sound like Lily.'

'Once the property was in her name, I tried to buy it. She refused again. But she came to me when she needed more money. It seemed the only way to get her out.'

She took a deep breath. 'I can see it would have been hard to shift her otherwise. Thank you for telling me this, Luca. It does help me understand a little better.'

'It is no excuse for the way I treated you.'

'I guess you were still mad at me for slapping you and walking out.'

'A little,' he admitted, until he saw her face and he

smiled ruefully. 'Maybe more than a little. But I have a confession to make about that time.' His hands squeezed hers, his fingers interlocking with hers. 'You bothered me that night, Valentina. You got under my skin. You were too perfect and you shouldn't have been—you were Lily's daughter after all and I didn't want to like you. I wanted somebody I could walk away from and I knew I couldn't stay away from you, unless you hated me.'

She shook her head, a frown tugging her fair brows together. 'And yet you did hold it against me.' But he took heart that her words weren't angry. Instead they searched for understanding amidst the tangle of revelations, as if she was searching for the one thread that would pull the knots free. He took heart that she was still listening and tried to find her the key.

'Because it suited me to. Don't you see? By blowing it out of proportion, by making it your fault, it gave me an excuse to get you to Venice, and to legitimise it by calling it vengeance. And it was easy to be angry, because I was mad at Lily for letting the house fall into such disrepair, and I hadn't forgotten you, and that made me even madder.

'I am sorry I said what I did. It was designed to drive you away. It was hurtful, just as the words I said before you left Venice were designed to hurt. And why? Because I needed to believe the worst of you, that you had destroyed our child.' He felt her flinch, as if reliving the pain of his accusations but he just squeezed her hands and pressed on. 'I'm so sorry. Because just as it worked that night we spent together, my ugly words worked only too well, and this time drove you from Venice.' He shrugged and looked up the hill towards the grave. 'I guess it is only just that I should be the one who paid some of the cost too, by never knowing of my son's existence until now.'

A wave crashed on the rocks below, sending spray high,

droplets that sparkled like diamonds in the thin sun before spinning into nothingness.

'I can never make up to you all the wrongs I have committed,' he said. 'I'm so sorry.'

For a few moments she said nothing, and he imagined that any time now she would pull her hands from his, thank him for his explanation and justifiably remove herself from his life once again. This time for good.

But her hands somehow remained in his. And then came her tentative question. 'Why did you need to drive me away so very badly?'

He looked into her eyes, those amber pools that he had come to love, along with their owner. 'Because otherwise I would have had to admit the truth. That I love you, Valentina. And I know you will not want to hear this from me—not after all that has happened—all that I have subjected you to. But I had to come and see you. I had to ask if there was any way you could ever forgive me.'

She looked up at him incredulously. 'You love me?'

He wasn't surprised she didn't believe him. It was a miracle she hadn't slapped him again for saying it. 'I do. I'm an idiot and a fool and every type of bastard for the things I've said to you and done to you, but I love you, Valentina, and I cannot bear the thought of you not being part of my life. When you left Venice, you took my heart with you. But I know I am clutching at straws. That you are too good for someone like me. That you deserve better. Much better.'

'You might be right,' she said, fresh tears springing from her eyes, and his freshly opened heart fell to his feet. 'Maybe I do deserve better. But damn you, Luca Barbarigo, it's you who I love. It's you I want to be with.'

Could a man die of happiness? he wondered as he cradled her face in his hands, letting her words seep through his consciousness, all the way through the layers of doubts and impossibilities, all the way through to his heart. 'Valentina,' he whispered, because there was nothing better he could think of to say, not when her lips were calling.

He loved her.

Tina could see it in his eyes, could feel it in his gentle touch. Could feel it in the shimmer of sea salt air between them and in the connection of his heart to hers.

Their lips meshed, the salt of their tears blending with the salt of the sea, and she tasted their shared loss and the heated promise of life and love.

'I love you,' he said. 'Oh God, it's taken too long to realise it, but I love you, Valentina. I know I don't deserve to ask this, but will you do me the honour of becoming my wife?'

His words, his rich voice, vibrated through her senses and her bones and found a joyful answer in her heart, her tears a rapturous celebration. 'Oh, Luca, yes! Yes, I will be your wife.'

He gathered her up and held her tight, so tight as he spun her around in the boom and spray from another crashing wave, that she felt part of him. She was part of him.

And when he put her down on her feet again, it was to look seriously into her eyes. 'Perhaps, after we are married, if you like, then maybe we could try again. For another child. A brother or sister for Leo.'

She shuddered in his arms. 'But what if…' He looked down at her with such an air of hope that it magnified her fear tenfold. 'I'm afraid, Luca,' she said, looking up the hill towards the plot where their one child already lay. 'Nobody knows why it happened and I don't think I could bear it if it happened again. I don't think I could come back from that.'

'No.' He rocked her then, wanting to soothe away her fears. 'No. It won't happen again.'

'How do you know that?'

'I don't. I wish to God I could promise you that it won't happen again, but I can't. But what I can promise you is this, that if it did happen again, if life chose to be so cruel again, that this time you would not be alone, that I will be there alongside you, holding your hand. And this time your loss would be my loss. Your tears would be my tears. I will never let you go through something like that alone again.'

The sheer power of his words gave her the confidence to believe him. The emotion behind his words gave her the courage to want to try.

'Perhaps,' she said plaintively, lifting her face to his, 'when we are married…'

And he growled at the courage of this woman and he pulled her close and kissed her again and held her tight, against the wind tugging at their clothing and the spray from the crashing waves—against the worst that life could throw at them.

And knew that whatever came their way, their love would endure for ever.

EPILOGUE

THEY were married in Venice, the wedding gondola decked out in black and crimson with highlights of gold. The cushions were made of silk and satin, the upholstery plush velvet. And while the gondolier himself looked resplendent in crisp attire, propelling the vessel with an effortless looking rhythm, it was to the bride sitting beaming alongside her proud father that every eye was drawn.

It was the bride from whom Luca couldn't tear his eyes.

His bride.

Valentina.

She stepped from the vessel in a gown befitting the goddess that she was, honey gold in colour, a timeless one-shouldered design, skimming her breasts before draping softly to the ground, both classic and feminine, the necklace of amber beads Luca had given her at her throat.

They married in the Scuola Grande di San Giovanni Evangelista, the opera house where they had seen *La Traviata*, the night Tina had felt the ground move beneath her feet and realised she had fallen in love with Luca. Her father gave her away, passing her hand to Luca's with a grudging smile, before taking his place in the front and curling his fingers possessively around those of his guest, none other than Deidre Turner. Tina smiled, happy for her father, happier for herself when the service began, the ceremony that would make her Luca's bride.

And if the wedding was magnificent, the reception was a celebration, held in the refurbished palazzo where Luca had grown up. Now restored to its former glory, its piers strengthened and renewed, its façade was as richly decorated as it once had been, befitting one of the oldest families in Venice.

'It's such a beautiful wedding,' said Lily to her daughter with a wistful sigh as the pair touched up their lipstick in the powder room together. 'But then you look beautiful, Valentina. I don't think I've ever seen such a radiant bride.'

Tina hadn't been able to stop smiling all day, but now her smile widened as she turned towards her mother. 'I love him, Lily. And I'm so very happy.'

Her mother took her daughter's hands in hers. 'It shows. I'm so proud of you, Valentina. You've grown into a wonderful woman, and I'm just sorry for all the grief I've caused you along the way. But I promise I will be a better mother to you—I am the same person, but I am trying to change, I am trying to be better.'

'Oh, Lily.' Tears sprang to her eyes and she blinked them away as Lily swung into action and passed her tissues before she tested the limits of her waterproof mascara.

'And now I've made you cry! *Sacre bleu!* That will not do. So let me tell you something instead to make you smile—Antonio was so moved, he proposed to me right after the ceremony.'

Tina gasped, her tears staunched by the surprise announcement. 'And?'

'I said yes, of course! I can't hope to change everything about me at once.' And then they were both reaching for the tissues, they were laughing so hard.

'Lily's agreed to marry Antonio,' she told Luca, as he

spun her around the ballroom's centuries-old terrazzo floor.

Luca smiled down at her. 'Do you think Mitch will agree to give her away too?'

'I don't know,' she reflected, as she watched her father spin past them with Deidre, their gazes well and truly locked. 'There's a good chance he might be otherwise *engaged*.'

Luca laughed, and hugged her closer. 'You don't mind then, that you might lose your father to another woman?'

'Not a chance. I'm happy for him. Besides—' she turned her face up to his '—look at all I've won. I must be the luckiest woman in the whole world.'

'I love you,' he said, whirling her around. 'I will always love you.'

His bride beamed up at him, felt her amber eyes misting. 'I love you too,' she pledged, 'with all my heart.'

His eyes darkened, his mouth drew closer, but she stilled him with a fingertip to his lips. 'But wait! That's not all I have to tell you. There's more.'

She leaned up closer to his ear and whispered the secret she'd been longing to share ever since she'd found out, and Luca responded the way she'd hoped, by whooping with joy as he spun her around the floor in his arms until she was drunk with giddiness. And then he stopped spinning and kissed her until she was giddy all over again, but this time on the love fizzing through her veins.

And both of them knew the day could not have been more perfect, and yet still it was nothing compared to what happened seven months later.

Mitchell Eduardo Barbarigo came into the world bang on time and boasting a healthy set of lungs. True to his word, Luca was by Tina's side, clutching her hand, sponging her brow or rubbing her back or just being there, the whole time. True to his word, she was not alone.

And just as true to his word, her tears were his tears, except this time they were tears of joy. Tears of elation.

Tears of love for this brand new family.

* * * * *

COMING NEXT MONTH from Harlequin Presents®

AVAILABLE FEBRUARY 19, 2013

#3121 PLAYING THE DUTIFUL WIFE

Carol Marinelli

When Meg Hamilton learns that her estranged husband, Niklas Dos Santos, needs her help she agrees, but only in exchange for his signature on the divorce papers. Except she hadn't bargained on their mind-blowing connection being as undeniable as ever.

#3122 A SCANDAL, A SECRET, A BABY

Sharon Kendrick

Wickedly sexy—and impossibly ruthless—Dante D'Arezzo is the last person Justina wants to see. He broke her heart once; she won't surrender to his insatiable desire again. But what Dante wants, he gets—no matter the consequences!

#3123 THE FALLEN GREEK BRIDE

The Disgraced Copelands

Jane Porter

Infamous Morgan Copeland's reputation is in tatters. Holding on to the last shreds of her pride, she must seek help from the most merciless man she knows... her husband, Drakon Xanthis. Her only bargaining chip? Her body!

#3124 A REPUTATION FOR REVENGE

Princes Untamed

Jennie Lucas

Revenge is at Kasimir's fingertips; the champagne is on ice and his new wife, Josie, waits in the bedroom—and victory has never tasted sweeter. But Josie's purity tests the one thing Kasimir didn't know he had—*honor.*

#3125 THE NOTORIOUS GABRIEL DIAZ
Cathy Williams

The last time Gabriel Diaz heard the word *no* was when Lucy Robins rejected his skilled advances. Now she stands before him offering a deal—but just how high a price will Gabriel expect, and is Lucy ready to pay it?

#3126 TAMING THE LAST ACOSTA
Susan Stephens

Living her life vicariously through her camera, photojournalist Romy Winner is happy to stay in the background.... Until former Argentinian polo champion turned Special Forces soldier Kruz Acosta challenges her to step out of the shadows—and into his bed!

#3127 CAPTIVE IN THE SPOTLIGHT
Annie West

Domenico Volpe's life has been paparazzi fodder for years...glitz, glamour and lastly a family tragedy. He's determined to keep Lucy Knight—the woman at the center of it all—quiet, even if that means locking her away with him on his island!

#3128 ISLAND OF SECRETS
Robyn Donald

Luc MacAllister believes Joanna Forman is a gold digger of the worst kind, but they need each other if they are to get their hands on their inheritance. Yet the sizzling attraction that burns between them threatens to ruin it all....

HPCNM0213RB

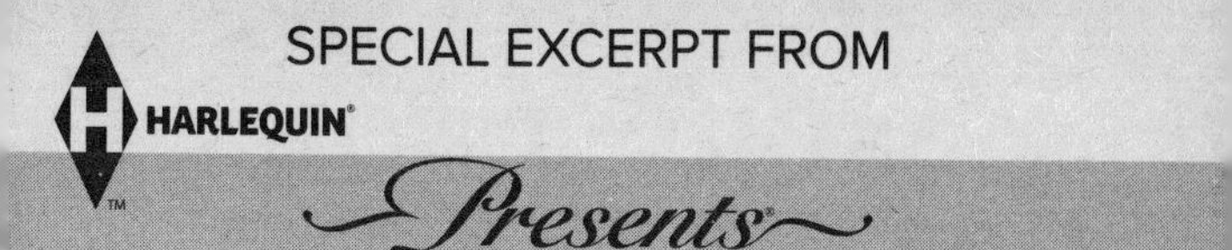

Life for the Copeland family was filled with unrivaled luxury—until scandalous allegations rocked their foundations, forcing Morgan Copeland to turn to the one man she never wanted to see again. Her husband!

Read on for an exciting excerpt from the first book in a fantastic new miniseries, THE DISGRACED COPELANDS, *by sensational author Jane Porter!*

* * *

HE was going to kiss her. And she wanted the kiss, craved his kiss, even as a little voice of reason inside her head sounded the alarm….

Stop. Wait. Think.

Morgan had to remember…remember the past…remember what had happened last time…. This wasn't just a kiss, but an inferno. If she gave in, it would be all over. Drakon was so dangerous for her. He did something to her. He, like his name, Drakon, Greek for dragon, was powerful, potent and destructive.

But he was also beautiful, physical and sensual. He made her feel. My God, he made her *feel,* and she wanted that intensity now.

"My beautiful, expensive mistake," he murmured, his lips brushing across the shell of her ear, making her breath catch in her throat and sending hot darts of delicious sensation throughout her body.

"Next time, don't marry the girl," she said, trying to sound brazen and cavalier but failing miserably.

"Would you have been happier as my mistress?" he asked, his tongue tracing the curve of her ear even as his muscular thigh pressed up, his knee against her core, teasing her senses, making her shiver with need. "Would you have been able to let go more? Enjoyed the sex without guilt?" he added, biting her tender earlobe, his teeth sharp, even as he wedged his thigh deeper between her knees.

"There was no guilt," she choked, eyes closing as he worked his thigh against her in a slow maddening circle. She knew it was wrong, but she wanted more, not less.

"Liar." He leaned in closer, his hips pressing down against her hips, making her feel hot. "You liked it hot. You liked it when I made you fall apart."

And it was true, she thought, her body so tight and hot and aching that she arched against him, absolutely wanton. There was no satisfaction like this, though, and she wanted satisfaction. Wanted him. Wanted him here and now.

* * *

Find out what price Drakon puts on Morgan's redemption in THE FALLEN GREEK BRIDE, available February 19, 2013, from Harlequin Presents®!

HPEXP0213-2